William Wilsey Martin

By Solent and Danube

Poems and Ballads

William Wilsey Martin

By Solent and Danube
Poems and Ballads

ISBN/EAN: 9783744787765

Printed in Europe, USA, Canada, Australia, Japan

Cover: Foto ©Andreas Hilbeck / pixelio.de

More available books at **www.hansebooks.com**

BY SOLENT AND DANUBE.

BY SOLENT AND DANUBE.

Poems and Ballads.

BY

W. WILSEY MARTIN.

LONDON:

TRÜBNER & CO., LUDGATE HILL.

1885.

Dedication.

TO MY DAUGHTER,

Ada Louise.

As earth greets sunshine with the golden gifts
Fed of its beams, would I, dear one, greet thee,
Who hast been sunshine to my heart and brain
Since thy sweet eyes first look'd upon our world.
  Earth gives the incense of her breathing flowers,
The hues of holiday, on bud and leaf,
The worship of her trees, the soaring songs
Of all her birds.—She gives her best, and I
Give these: the wrinkled leaves, the struggling blooms
Of thought, stirr'd in the air of poesy,
And blossoming upon that side of me
Which loves thy sunshine, and the light of home.

  August 1885.

CONTENTS.

—+—

BY THE SOLENT.

𝕽𝖔𝖓𝖉𝖊𝖆𝖚𝖝.

𝕾𝖔𝖓𝖓𝖊𝖙𝖘.

Quatrains.

Songs.

BY THE DANUBE.

MISCELLANEOUS.

By the Solent.

A GOLDEN DAY.

I.

THE sunbeams filter through the pines
    And tangled undermass ;
But kinglike, through the aspen-trees
    In golden splendour pass ;
And the shadows of the moving leaves
    Chequer the tender grass.

A shade-loved bank slopes near, thorn-topp'd,
    With straggling brambles wild,
Where lurks, the last of all the year,
    A primrose faint and mild ;
'Mid laughing speedwell bright with eyes,
    The blue eyes of a child.

A

The cranesbill lifts a saucy face,
    A red flag gleams afar,
Fit flag for fairy-elves to bear
    O'er bank, and bush, and scar;
While stitchwort white peeps here and there,
    And twinkles like a star.

II.

O wild flowers of my motherland!
    Gems of the woodland wide,
Companions in our burden'd ways,
    Meek watchers by our side;
What tender thoughts, from birth to age,
    Within your petals hide.

The toddling pet with dimpled hands,
    Among the meadow daisies,
Will clutch their silver and their gold,
    And scream his treble praises;
While Age amid the leaves will track
    Green memory's shadowy mazes.

The trefoil of our early youth
    With silver dewdrops wet;
The hue of Love's forget-me-nots,
    We never can forget—

The perfume of those violets blue
    Is floating round us yet.

'Twas not an English hot-house plant *
    That, sent across the seas,
Evoked a welcome warm and wild
    In the far antipodes,
That stirr'd to life in distant hearts
    The old-home sympathies—

No, 'twas an English primrose pale
    That made their bosoms glow;
A yellow primrose from the wood
    That made their warm tears flow;
A primrose, from the old loved land,
    The misty long-ago.

The human heart is wayward, strange,
    Uncertain flow its springs,
But ever bound by simplest ties,
    And link'd to simplest things;
A song—a lock of hair—a flower,
    Will touch its tenderest strings.

---

* Dr. Ward mentioned in a paper read at the Royal Institution, that a primrose had, in the early days of the colony, been taken to Australia in a covered glass case ; and when it arrived there in full bloom, the sensation it excited as a remembrance from the old Fatherland was so great, that it was found necessary to protect it with a strong guard.

III.

Ah! what is this? a dead leaf falls,
    A leaf of last year's green
Floats gently here from yon tall beech,
    And whispers—"I have been;
And thou, like me, wilt bloom thy bloom,
    And then be no more seen."

Thanks, little leaf! thou preachest well,
    To me, no sadden'd strain;
Both man and leaf are mystic links
    In Nature's endless chain—
If I fulfil myself, as thou,
    I shall not live in vain.

Long life was thine, thou sturdy leaf,
    For many days have been
Since first the wooing voice of Spring
    Enticed thee on the scene—
Thy heart, responsive, burst the bud,
    And she beheld thee green.

Thy fellow-gladdeners of the wood,
    Thy brothers—where are they?
Some overkist by Summer, fell,
    And some by slow decay,

And some by fierce Autumnal winds
    And storms were swept away.

But thou held'st on—O gallant leaf!
    Through hurtling hail and snow,
The hurricane's tempestuous breath,
    The lightning's angry glow:
Nor did'st thou fall, till this year's leaves
    Told thee 'twas time to go.

Go, little leaf, and take thy rest,
    Thy tiny flag is furl'd;
Thou'rt old, and dry, and stiff with age,
    And russet-red and curl'd;
But in thy day thou did'st thy best
    To beautify the world!

IV.

So still I sit, a robin chirps
    And flutters near my feet;
Now watches, sidelong, 'mid the boughs
    That gloom my rustic seat;
While the linden hums her wing-made song
    In slumb'rous summer heat.

Huge Alp-lands of sun-smitten clouds
    On the horizon lie,

And rear their silver battlements
   Into the windless sky—
Vast regions of untroubled calm
   Beyond the human cry.

And overhead, scarce one stray film
   To fleck the tender blue;
And in my heart, scarce one stray care
   To cloud the spirit's hue,
For the beauty of the scene hath sooth'd
   And fill'd me through and through.

V.

O Nature, how I love thy ways!
   Unsullied, fresh and free,
Be they within the solemn woods,
   Or by the restless sea,
On hillside, underneath the stars,
   Or clover-scented lea—

To me the same, where'er they lead
   Remote from crowded street,
Where, caged and bound, I often pine
   For rest in thy retreat;
To look thee closer in the face,
   And worship at thy feet.

Health lives upon the breezy downs,
    Where the bending harebell blows,
Young hope lies hid in shining leaves —
    A balm for mental woes—
And in the foldings of a flower,
    The heart may fiud repose.

VI.

Now smiles the far coast in its sleep,
    The Solent rolls serene,
Streak'd here with tints of greenest blue,
    And there of bluest green,
And there of purple lost in grey
    And silver'd in between.

The sense that I have nought to do
    Steals sweetly over me;
Nothing to do for one green month,
    Nothing to do—but be—
To lie full length on grassy slope
    In sight of summer sea.

To weary worker forced to seek
    The feathers for his nest;
To toiling, moiling, busy ones,
    How good a thing is rest!

The Peace that falls from Angels' wings
   On eyelids of the blest.

Some roads may pass through level ways,
   And they who tread repine
That in the vale they cannot trace
   The far horizon line,
That life is strife for daily bread,
   With little oil and wine.

Yet work, methinks, gives ampler range;
   And paths, though flat and grey,
May lead to rosy heights at last
   When duty points the way;
For labour makes a king of man,
   And crowns him every day.

VII.

O golden hours of vagrant thought!
   Unbent the daily strain—
Shut out the calling, writing world,
   The care of loss or gain—
Rest for the eyelids and the eyes,
   Rest for the hand and brain.

The glories of all summer days
   My soul hath made its own;

The fulness of all leisure-time
   My life hath ever known,
Come back in this, on heart and mind,
   Like some remember'd tone,—

Some tone heard down the glades of time
   (Perchance in other spheres),
Whose recognition floods the soul
   As it falls upon the ears,
With feelings closely link'd with joy,
   Yet half akin to tears.

I would this hour could stretch itself
   Along my future ways;
Its peace, with all her wings, enfold
   My life in after days,
Ere old age totters to the brink
   Encrown'd with silver haze.

VIII.

See now! the shadows of the trees
   Are lengthen'd on the grass;
In distant reaches gleams the sea
   A flood of floating glass;
And white sails flash like sea-birds' wings
   As round the Point they pass.

The golden sun is half immersed
   Beneath the lucent sea,
And greater, in the parting smile,
   His bright face seems to be—
E'en as our good gifts larger grow
   The moment ere they flee.

A glorious sunset! cirrus clouds,
   The ringlets of the sky,
Shake out their tresses flush'd with gold
   And hues that blend and die;
While loom, like mountains fringed with light,
   The giant cumuli.

IX.

Still, still I muse, till silvery stars
   Hang out their fires on high;
And earth-born lights from ship and shore
   Give answer to the sky;
And gleam, from twice a hundred barks,
   In spangled broidery.

God hangs His lamps in heaven above,
   Man lights his lamps below;
To me—a sweet mysterious link
   With destinies that glow,

And roll in music past all thought
  Or human passions' flow.

The white breast of the tranquil sea
  Reflects both lights together;
The one, majestic, calm, sublime,
  One flickering, wavering ever—
Emblems of God's eternal love,
  And feeble man's endeavour.

The lichen-coated moths brush past
  To greet our window's light—
'Tis time to rise—the wind begins
  A storm-song to the night;
And voices call me, faces peep,
  Small faces pink and white.

Farewell, sweet time! farewell, sweet thoughts!
  I hide your light away
Within my memory-cells, perchance,
  To glad me when I'm grey,—
And in the diary of my life
  Mark this a golden day.

CROSSING.

I LAY afloat, in an idle boat
  (A fisher-lad held the oar),
Off a Devon strand, and watch'd the grand
  Old sea run up the shore.

The Welsh coast slept, where the waters crept
  Far out on the utmost rim ;
Slept with its pines, in long, low lines,
  Shadowy, grey, and dim.

Old Lundy lay some leagues away,
  Guarding the middle sea ;
A silver mist his low length kist,
  Yet rugged and cold look'd he.

And there, as I lay in that slate-bound bay,
   While that fisher-lad sat by me,
A butterfly came, with wings aflame,
   Fluttering out to sea.

From heather and broom, like a wingèd bloom,
   From fields where the charlock grew,
From cowslip cells, and hyacinth bells,
   Over the foam he flew.

Does he seek a bride, on that far Welsh side?
   Does he dream, as he wanders o'er,
Of fairer flowers, and sunnier hours,
   And love on a golden shore?

Does the wee thing own a sense unknown
   To us, who are Nature's kings?
Can he hear the beat of his love's fair feet,
   And the pulse of her luminous wings?

" Come back," I cry, " frail butterfly,
   Come back to the land, and live!
Each cup of the fields rare nectar yields,
   But what hath the sea to give?"

Still on he flies—I strain mine eyes—
   " O fisher-lad, raise the mast;

The wind is hale, so set thy sail,
   And follow far and fast."

We follow the flight of that thing of light,
   Under the blue serene,
With only the flow of the tide below,
   And only the wind between.

Now over the foam, as seeking a home
   In those cruel white blooms of the spray ;
Now seeming to rest on a wave's curl'd crest,
   And now up in the air, and away !

And ever he flew, and farther drew
   From the fast-receding shore :
And ever we sped, but ever he fled
   Fluttering on before.

" Turn, little one, turn where the clovers burn,
   Where the speedwell waits in the lane,
To greet thee with eyes like April skies,
   When April is on the wane.

" Though wondrous to thee are the fields of the sea,
   Though the foam-flowers lightly blow,
Beware of their breath, there is death, chill death,
   In the kiss of their tossing snow !

" Though the deeps laugh fair in the sunny air,
　And the arm of the wind is strong,
Thou wilt find no rest in gulf or crest,
　And the way is so long, so long!

" Stay, little one, stay!"　But no backward way
　Will those delicate wings pursue;
They throb through the haze, and part from my
　　gaze,
　Absorbed in the infinite blue.

And whether they pass'd to that shore at last,
　That shore beyond the sea,
Or found a grave in the purple wave,
　Can never be known to me.

　　.　　.　　.　　.　　.　　.　　.

Far lies the goal of the human soul,
　And frail are the wings for flight,
And the way is so wide, and fierce is the tide,
　And over all cometh the night.

STILL LOOKING.

By the weed-strewn, brown, desolate reaches,
   Lonely, and half broken-hearted,
     We met, and we parted,
By the weed-strewn, brown, desolate reaches.

A moan from the dolorous ocean
   Crept round about and above her—
     To the ear of each lover
Crept a moan from the dolorous ocean.

The dun cormorant rustled above us;
   Her dissonant cry boded evil;
     Like goblin or devil,
The dun cormorant rustled above us.

One wild clinging kiss, and we parted,
  No light fringed the skirts of our morrow;
    In silence, in sorrow,
One wild clinging kiss, and we parted.

We turned, face to face, stepping backward,
  The distance between us grew wider;
    Ere distance could hide her,
We turned, face to face, stepping backward.

The mists weird and white came between us,
  As a screen, parting one from the other;
    Parting lover from lover,
The mists weird and white came between us.

Yet I know my old love is still looking
  'Thwart the gloom of the years as they follow,
    With eyes sad and hollow;
I know my old love is still looking.

Rondeau.

JASMINE STARS.

WHITE Jasmine stars, upon an old grey wall,
Whereon the yellow sunbeams seldom fall,
Rain-stain'd and weather-worn, yet wholly fair,
For one lush creeper clings in greenness there,
With dark-hued leaves and blossoms white and small.

It was a loving hand o'er that old wall
First taught the young arms of the Jasmine tall
To cling, and spread star-clusters everywhere.
    Sweet Jasmine stars!

When my lone heart was cold as yon grey wall,
A little Jasmine came, at Love's low call,
And warm'd with starry blooms the chambers bare;
My heart grew glad, and the impassion'd air
Pierced with its fragrance spread it over all.
    O Jasmine stars!

SLEEP, BABY MINE.

SLEEP, baby mine. The failing light is low,
The witch-elms toss their branches to and fro ;
And howling winds sing baby's lullaby.
Move, shadows move, and grey frost-clouds go by,
My baby sleeps, whatever winds may blow.

Sleep, baby mine ; while he, who loves us so,
Is daring all the bitter, drifting snow
Across the moorlands where the great winds cry.
        Sleep, baby mine !

Within—The crackling wood-fire's ruddy glow
Warms each wee hand, and curlèd roseleaf toe.
Without—The blinding, biting storm mounts high,
And barbèd snowflakes scatter down the sky.
God send thy father ere the darkness grow !
        Sleep, baby mine !

BLOW, WILD MARCH WIND.

BLOW, wild March wind!   In hollows of the lea,
In copses low, thy bride awaiteth thee—
The timid, saint-like, white anemone.
She will not show her face, though woo'd by kings,
Till o'er her beat the pulsings of thy wings.

Blow, wild March wind! that we her face may
    see,
Through pine-clad gorges by our northward sea,
Through English woodlands where the blackcap sings.
               Blow, wild March wind!

She lifts her face.   The answering passion stings
Her veinèd leaves, at the rough kiss he brings.

Sing round her bridal couch thy melody,
Thy breath is life to her.   Apart from thee
She droops and dies, the frailest of frail things—
            Then blow, March wind!

SWEET LAGGARD, COME.

—⧐—

SWEET laggard, come! and list the drowsy chime
Of happy bees, 'neath umbrage of the lime—
The Spring is here, come thou and be my Spring!

The trees put on their leaves while west-winds sing,
Do thou put on the love my heart doth bring.

Sweet laggard, come! Waste not the vernal time,
Enjoy the breath of Love's delicious prime—
The Spring is here, come thou and be my Spring!
            Sweet laggard, come!

The golden wren doth like a blossom swing,
And hark! the curlews clamour on the wing.

Sweet laggard, come! and list thy lover's rhyme,
As up the starry ways of love we climb,
Thou queen of all my song, and I thy king.
            Sweet laggard, come!

TWIT TWIT, TWIT TWIT.

Twit twit, twit twit!   The martins come again,
With wings aweary, flying o'er the main
From Senegal or dry Morocco's shore.

Snow-breasted exiles! seek your homes once more,
Each last year's nest still shows an open door.

Twit twit, twit twit!   The martins come again,
Underneath my eaves, above my window-pane ;
They bring me all the Spring in their low strain,
                    Twit twit, twit twit!

Blithe birds of mystery—God-taught—give o'er
Your tireless flight, and teach me half your lore.

Now, black against the sapphire sky they soar,
Now, flash with white athwart the April rain,
Returning ever with the low refrain,
                    Twit twit, twit twit!

THE AUTUMN LEAVES GO BY.

—*+*—

THE autumn leaves, the autumn leaves go by,
In gusty showers of red and gold they fly;
In showers of brown and grey sink low to die.

The old leaves fall not till the buds be born;
And Love's bud lives, though last year's hopes lie
    shorn.

Wind answers wind with melancholy cry;
The branches lift bare lances to the sky,—
And all my heart is bare, and cold, and dry
         As autumn leaves.

O maiden with the amber hair of morn!
Kill not Love's autumn bud with frosts of scorn.

Come, autumn leaves! and cover from the eye
Of day my germ of love, till spring winds sigh;
For young hope lives, tho' old hopes lowly lie
         As autumn leaves.

THE AUTUMN LEAVES LIE DEAD.

THE autumn leaves, the autumn leaves lie dead;
But through the swaying bough-rifts looks the blue,
And I see more of Heaven overhead.

My joys were summer leaves; so thick they grew,
That Heaven's sweet light could only filter through.

The autumn leaves, the autumn leaves lie dead,
My joys are trampled leaves, and lost to view;
The winds that took them brought me grief instead.
O autumn leaves!

My joys Love could not keep when strong storms
blew;
Love could but weep, because they were so few.

All hues have died, grey, gold, and russet-red.
The lacing boughs form windows o'er my head,
And through each one, God's light is shining true,
Though autumn leaves lie dead.

Sonnet.

— ⋅⋈⋅ —

THE PEARL OF PEACE.

A BIVALVE feeding in the warm salt sea
   Draws inward, with the wave, a sandy grain,
   Which, not returning with the wave again,
Remains henceforth its secret grief to be.
Day after day, so sea-wise folk agree,
   The creature hides it in a dew-like rain
   Of ceaseless tears, till, harden'd out of pain,
A precious pearl is fashion'd perfectly.

From outer seas of passion, seas of strife,
   There drifts at times upon the human heart
   A secret rankling grief that day by day
We cover with the bitter tears of life,
   Till, wrought of pain from out our nobler part,
   The pearl of Peace remains with us alway.

A WILD NIGHT.

HARK! at the front door knocks the wintry blast,
  Angry and loud, as one that will be heard:
  Fair Nature, from her sleep uncouthly stirr'd,
Writhes in the storm; the raindrops patter fast,
Crash follows crash, each louder than the last;
  Above the hills resounds the gathering word
  Of warlike winds, that now to madness spurr'd,
Against the windows hailshafts thickly cast,
  So thick, that Fancy, on the whirlwind, sees
A troop of storm-imps, who, amid the rain,
  Bear up, for mischief, granaries of peas,
And dash quick handfuls 'gainst the window-pane.
  In vain I strive to compass slumb'rous ease,
Sleep will not settle on my wakeful brain.

THE WOOING OF THE MOON AND SEA.

THE moon is woo'd by her wild lord the sea,
　　Whose yearning waves wax wanton in their joy,
　　Upheaving amorously; he fain would toy
With his sweet moon, as I would toy with thee.

In long low sighs he uttereth his plea;
　　She half unveils her face, as maiden coy,
　　Then beams her love; he doth the winds employ
To messenger his speech, while listeneth she.

Her image in his breast she sees to-night
　　In broken gold, whene'er his voice is rough;
So thou may'st see thy face of moon-pale light
　　In my true eyes, if thou look close enough.
She draws her sea's deep heart.　Thou draw'st thy
　　　　knight,
　　Whose heart-tide sets to thee, nor fears rebuff.

TO ———.

THERE dwells sweet music in her speaking face,
    And 'neath the curtains of her sea-grey eyes
    Her soul looks out, as 'mid the dappled skies
Looks forth the blue.   And I have loved to trace
Thought chasing thought with ever-shifting pace,
    O'er face and brow wherein all discord dies;
    To watch each sun-lit smile, that breaking, flies,
Or finds around her perfect mouth its place.
Nor grave is she, nor is she passing gay;
    But, as the iris-colours blend in air,
So all her moods do blend in her alway—
    So womanlike withal—so young, so fair,
Thrice happy he who in a golden day
    Wins her, to climb with him life's rugged stair.

POWER.

—⋆—

SELF-RULE sustain'd, the sovereignty of will,
  With reverence of self and manhood fraught,
  Controlling action and each prompting thought,
The knowledge of himself for good and ill
Give man a force o'er man—to strive until
  He finds the light; until the dews are caught
  From ancient mists on awful heights, and brought
To parchèd lips, constrained to take their fill.

As beacons on the mountains, towering, grand,
  Stand out the master-minds in shine and shower,
Old Time's grey cheek hath wrinkled since they
      plann'd
  And wrought for human weal.—Their deathless
      dower
The ages pay, whose homage they command,
  And wield, with forceful sway, a Godlike power!

THE MISTLETOE BOUGH.

I.

Wave, mystic bough, with all thy pearls;
  Shine, little pearls, o'er bench and stall,
  In poor man's cottage, rich man's hall;
Make glad our English boys and girls.

And gladden us of longer years,
  Made children by thy happy glow,
  Recalling from the long-ago
Dead kisses and forgotten tears.

We weave thy tints with those that gleam
  More bravely in the holly sprays,
  And weaving, muse of ancient days,
And musing, see as those who dream.

The forest glades, the solemn night,
　The glory where the moonbeams slant,
　The Druids' weird unearthly chant,
The glinting robes—the pagan rite.

And then from out the darkness leaps
　A light—around the holly borne—
　A light that on that Christmas morn
First broke upon Judæan steeps.

In golden shafts which flush'd the wind
　With glory, borne o'er every sea,
　The herald of great good to be—
Freedom and hope for human kind.

II.

Wave, mystic bough! To thee belong
　The praises that I fain would sing;
　From out the wintry woodlands bring
The gladness of thy thrush's song.

The foliage died on bank and byre,
　The pale leaves flutter'd, stricken dead;
　The rain-clouds gather'd overhead,
The West was lit with sullen fire.

Each tree drew on its snowy hood,
    Or bared gaunt arms, whilst thou between
    Didst shine, a flash of golden green
Upon the darkness of the wood.

Shine now on all our darken'd days,
    On hearth and home, on young and old,
    And teach some hearts to fling their gold,
As thou thy light, in straiten'd ways.

Shine now, that underneath thy leaves
    The custom old may live anew,
    And kisses fall, when hearts are true,
As plentiful as autumn sheaves.

Shine out on all, and far and wide—
    On cheeks where lingers yet the tear,
    On hearts so weary of the year—
A flash of joy this Christmas-tide !

THE BIRTH OF THE RED-ROSE.

(HENDECASYLLABICS.)

THRO' the gateways of Eden, Eve all mournful
Look'd, gold gateways of Eden, sharply closing
On our mother, who laving with wet sorrow
Her soul's bitterness, loth to leave her bower,
Whose cool leaflets and tendrils barr'd the sunbeams,
Saw her home of the future, in the distance,
Bare, wild, cheerless, beset with leafless branches,
Thorns, sharp thistles and horrid growths unsightly,
No buds broke to the hills where Heaven slumber'd,
For the flowerless plain was parch'd and barren ;
So she pray'd to the bright, the guarding Angel :
" O wing'd spirit ! as good as thou art lovely,
Grant me time yet to linger 'mid my flowers,
Time to gather the seed-cells of my blossoms ;
Ere we bear to the wilds our weight of weeping."

Then fair Eve to her garden sped, half-cheerful ;
In her hasting her lithe limbs shook a snowfall

C

Of white rose-leaves.   The small gales caught her
  tresses ;
The clear stream, at her fair flesh, rippled wonder ;
Pards, large-eyed, as she pass'd by look'd allegiance;
Love-torn creepers caress'd her with their tendrils ;
The green sward, at her tread, with daisies silver'd ;
Pale proud lilies low-bow'd their heads—she pass-
  ing—
For the souls of the flowers felt her presence,
As the earth the sweet whisper of the spring-time.

Love-lured airs with low music palpitated,
While white seraphs, above her, sang their greetings :
"Thy seed shall in the ages crush the serpent."
Sang they Hope, and fair Faith, and Love triumphant.
Once more rapture, ambrosïal, delightful,
Fill'd her heart, as the sunbeam fills the crocus ;
Wan-eyed Sorrow in sleep her pinions folded—
Wee bright cherubs, on rosy winglets, help'd her,
Brought her fruit of the bough, and seed of blos-
  som ;
Wealth of sun-woven fabrics—many-tinted
Cups of Paradise, full to brim with summer.

But a cry, as of pain, arose in Eden—
A sharp cry from the lips of Eve, embower'd
'Mid her roses, she, plucking milky blossoms,

Felt thorns twain, on a sudden, smite her finger;
Sharp thorns, sharper than spears, the first in Eden;
For the roses were thornless, smooth as willow,
Ere her sinfulness. Blood-drops stain'd the petals,
Erst as white as the hellebore in winter;
And she, musing, beheld a wondrous marvel—
Where the beads of her blood the leaves ensanguin'd,
Lo! red roses were born, as joys in sorrow,
A rose, red as the nut-tree bloom in spring-days.

'Neath the eaves of her argent lids, night-fringèd,
Twin tears wander'd adown her cheeks like lost
    stars,
Spheres of light, to the golden-hearted roses
Where they rested; and blossoms, erewhile scentless,
Gave an odour to sweeten all the ages.

In green shadowy ways, half glad, half mournful,
Mov'd fair Eve; and her consort watch'd her
    coming,
As peaks, swathed in the night-clouds, watch for
    morning.
Light she stept, with her flower-load uplifted,
Full ripe pendulous clusters bearing seed-pods,
Through the arches and aisles of leafy Eden.
Cheer'd she him, her belov'd, with smiles of sun-
    light,

He, our Father, was dark at heart and downcast;
But the glow of her presence flush'd his pulses,
And he fed on her face as one a-hunger'd.
Swung her burthen of scents upon his shoulder,
And, with arm on her white waist, pass'd the portals,
To the wilderness pass'd they, while behind them
Rang the dissonant clang of gates sharp closing.

Wander'd they in the wilds and desert places,
Till they reach'd, through a break among the moun-
    tains,
Way-worn, weary, a valley speck'd with verdure.
With swift silver the streamlets slash'd the hillsides
Worn with storms, and at last, in one stream
    gather'd,
Flow'd out, under the sun, to seek Euphrates.
There the exiles, heart-lighten'd, found a refuge,
Where, by labour of hands, uprose a garden,
Whose leaves sang in the wind of bygone pleasures.
There Eve sow'd in the earth the seeds of Eden,
And soon flowers, as flames of fire, brake upward,
Bright buds, splendid as those in Angels' garlands,
Guests in Paradise ere the curse resounded.

Through the mists of the years, each bloom she
    gathered,
Each seed's mystery, comes with tear-wet petals,

With the breath of the morn of earth, to woo us—
Comes, all stainless, to tell of days once sinless,
To point us where the star-buds bloom immortal.

Thanks, fair Mother of ours ! amid the shadows
That gloom us, and the tears that spring from
  sorrow,
Comes the thought, to our worn hearts bringing
  sweetness,
Buds from Paradise still adorn our pathways,
The pure blossoms of Eden cluster round us.

WAU-NE-BE-WIN-KA.

—⊶—

"Hence! come not near, let me die," said the Prin-
 cess, fair Wau-ne-be-win-ka.
" Death I prefer to the loss of a limb—yea, death;
 though the promise
Of youth is bright to my sight, and the path of the
 years is undarken'd.
Could I, the daughter of Wongo, King of the great
 Winnebagoes—
Could I lag lame in the forests and live ? could I
 limp as a cripple ?
I, call'd the Fleet of Foot, pride of the hunters, a
 red-doe in swiftness ?
Better is death than dishonour, and better than life
 as a cripple."
Thrust she then from her the Medas, and cut the
 loose flesh from her ankle,
Bound it up, bleeding and torn, badly crush'd to
 the bone in Wisconsin.

" Great is my daughter of heart," said the King of
    the tribe Winnebago ;

" Better a Princess should die, than be humbled by
    limping on crutches ;—

Hard for my child to die in the bloom of her youth
    and her beauty ;

Harder for me, O my sunshine ! left darkly to creep
    to my fathers.

Through the lush forest and prairie, a red fawn she
    gamboll'd beside me,

Liv'd in my heart, kept it flesh—as flint will it
    harden without her.

Through all the land was her voice as the breath of
    a song to my people ;

Songless and sad all the land, on the day that it
    sinks into silence.

Yield to the Medas and die not ! Stay with me,
    stay with the old man ! "

Turn'd then, pain-laden, the Princess, and answer'd,
    her eyes on her Father—

" Better is death than dishonour, and better than
    life as a cripple."

" Come to thy little-one, come ! " said the Princess
    Wau-ne-be-win-ka.

" Take my hand, O my Father ! dark Pan-guk is
    breathing upon me.

Raise my head with thine arm; let me gaze once
 more on the forest;
Now to the sky-woods it spreads, one forest from
 earth unto Heaven—
Golden and purpling in splendour stretch further
 the plains of the hunters.
Voices are calling and singing; the ghosts of our
 people are calling,
Calling my spirit to bound through the limitless
 prairie of Heaven—
Kiss me, my Father! I go!"

      "Nay, stay with me—stay !"
cried the old man.
Soft as the sigh of the trees in the tender calm of
 the evening,
Sweet as the moan of doves rose the last words of
 Wau-ne-be-win-ka—
" Better is death than dishonour, and better than
 life as a cripple."

" Great was my daughter of heart," said the King
 of the tribe Winnebago,
" Great, as a Princess should be, a Princess, the
 daughter of Wongo;
Fair as the flower of night, dew-wet 'neath the
 moon of green leaflets,

True as string to the bow, when bent by the arms of
the hunter.

Gone is my pretty one, gone, as the mist-wreath
caught up by the sunbeam—

Gone to our people above, in the fair summer Isles
of the Blessed—

Gone to the Home of the Light, the hills of the
Home of the Morning."

Wailing and weeping they bear her, the Princess
Wau-ne-be-win-ka.

Clothed in her robes of ermine, and deck'd in her
bead-work and tassels—

Wailing and weeping they bury her, deep in the
heart of the forest.

Bracelets and trinkets they place on the grave of
their lov'd one departed,

Belts of white wampum and furs, while a Brave
sings the song of her virtues.

Long will her last words live in the memory-cells
of her people—

" Better is death than dishonour, and better than
life as a cripple."

WILD FLOWERS.

WILD jocund flowers ! wee stars that spangle
  earth,
Shine on and twinkle in your verdant spheres.
Fabrics of light ! wrought in the looms of
  Heaven,
And painted with the pencil of a God.
O cheery little stars ! your gleaming rays,
From out the hedgerows and beside my path,
When stumbling in the mists, have often proved
So many friendly lights to guide me on.
I love to hold you by your slender stems,
And learn the golden lore within your eyes ;
Or, when ye swing your censers as ye pray
At eventide, upon my spirit's ear
To catch the voicings of your trembling choirs ;
Inhale your incense as it soars to God,
And feel I have a part with you. 'Tis good
To trace His impress on your veinèd leaves,
To track the filmy foldings of a rose,
Or gaze in silence on a daisy's fringe.

THE WHITE ROSE.

THE bride, a white rose with no flush of red,
   Moves down with all her maids, sweet jasmine
      stars;
   The best-man only sees the Altar bars;
He feels the white-rose thorn; and would be dead.

He hides his wound; he lifts a noble name
   For men to worship in the coming days;
   But dearer far to him than human praise
Is one fair face, and hair of yellow flame.

He bows his head beside a sculptured stone;
   The white rose sleeps; the thorn has ceased to
      pain;
   The perfumes only of the leaves remain.
He claims his dead, for ever his alone.

A VILLA in the South.   A lake that laves
   The marble terraces, whose orange-trees
Shake dewy odours over silver waves,
     Fann'd by a languid breeze.

I rest, half dreaming, watching 'neath my feet
   The slowly-gliding swans divide the mere—
A rustle, and a voice most clear and sweet
     Steals softly on mine ear.

"You know what I have come for.   His ship sails
   To-morrow—I must answer Yes or No—
And she won't hear of it."   The young voice fails,
     Then speaks again more low.

"But you will make me happy?   I should die
   If we were parted.   He so good, so true,
So generous: and he loves me so, and I—
     I love him dearly, too!"

A silence and a kiss, and round my neck
 Two white arms twine themselves, as if to win
Compliance from my yielding heart, and check
 The sterner thoughts within.

In such a strait, what could a father say ?
 A coaxing whisper—"Think of one whole
   year
That we have waited. Can he go away
 Without a word of cheer ? "

" Sweet daughter mine, bear with me if I seem,
 In love of you, to play a miser's part;
'Tis hard to speed a treasure down the stream
 Long hoarded in my heart.

" Is he so true and wise ? " " So wise, so true ! "
 " And can you trust yourself ? " " Beneath the
   sun
I know there is for me (not counting you)
 One only—only one ! "

" Well, well, no tears ! Methinks I never met
 An abler pleader—parting good from ill.
I would it were, and would it were not. Yet
 You conquer ; have your will."

Another kiss, another soft caress—
    She glides away, as sunlight thro' the flow'rs.
I sit and muse ; the winds in idleness
    Ruffle the orange bow'rs.

" Two hearts made happy, so what need to frown ?
    The children love each other. Smile, then, wife.
A happy love is sure the fairest crown
    And whitest flower of life."

Quatrains.

AMBITION.

THE royal eagle hawketh not for flies,
    Nor mates the soaring skylark with the wren;
    So, scorning narrow aims of lesser men,
Move to their goal, the minds of high emprise.

WORSHIP.

I WORSHIP Him who dwells anear, afar,
    Below the crocus breaking through the mould,
    Above the cloud-ships with their sails of gold,
Behind the protoplasm and the star.

FRIENDSHIP.

I.

SOME Friendships are like leaves; when skies are fair
  Their green flags flutter, making glad the day;
  But when the chill winds blow, they fall away
And leave the quiv'ring branches cold and bare.

II.

BREAK not an ancient Friendship; keep it hale;
  Stir round its roots, that it be green of heart;
  Let not the spirit of its growth depart:
It is a power to brave the strongest gale.

LOVE.

LOVE must be first and last, the part, the whole;
  Must fill the human void as ocean fills
  Its broadest channels, ancient as the hills,
And slightest shell o'er which its waters roll.

LOVE, HATE, FEAR.

I.

True love hath sight, but thro' a crystal spies,
   All flush'd with rosy light, its heart's desire;
   Fell hate glares through one lidless orb of fire;
But pallid fear hath twice a hundred eyes.

II.

The love of half a world may not avail
   To guard the hero from the secret thrust
   Of one mean foe; the brightest steel may rust,
And hate find chinks in coat of provèd mail.

FEAR NONE—FEAR ONE.

Of all mankind, there is but one
Whom thou shouldst fear beneath the sun—
In love or hate, for pride or pelf—
One—only one; that one—thyself!

D

HOPE.

I.

When Hope's glad sun shines full upon our track,
  We feel not much the burthen of our load;
  The light is in our face along the road,
And all the shadows lie behind our back.

II.

Hope is a dream whose climbing fancies take
  Their tincture from the iris-colour'd skies;
  A dream we ever dream with open eyes,
With hearts aglow, and senses all awake.

III.

Build palace halls! build castles in the air!
  Flush all their cloudy heights with rosy bloom!
  But raise no prison turreted in gloom,
And dig no cave to prove a wild beast's lair.

GRIEF.

GRIEF comes, a giantess, with strength to bind;
   She grips our hand and glares into our eyes;
   If we but kiss her mouth, she daily dies,
Fades into air, and leaves a flower behind.

MIRTH.

MIRTH comes, a reveller beneath the moon.
   Bring music! wine! Fling garlands on the floor!
   The guest withal is looking at the door—
The flow'rs he brings are cut, and wither soon.

TASTE.

FIVE senses fall to us from Nature's hand;
   But who shall say that some, more amply blest,
   Have not a sixth, controlling all the rest?
Taste is innate, not purchased at command.

LABOUR.

I.

LABOUR of brain, and of the good right hand,
   Gives man the mastership of half his fate ;
   Will crown him king for guerdon, soon or late,
With crown no royal idler can command.

II.

A garden is the mind, within whose bound
   You gather roses, but with horny hand.
   Who will not toil, no roses may command,
For thankless weeds will revel in the ground.

III.

I am not sure that life, to any one,
   A fuller measure of contentment brings,
    With all its gifts, than in the draught which
      springs
From honest work, well plann'd, and bravely done.

ENVY.

I.

THE envious man is sensitive of sight;
  Some sounds, too, fret his ear, as light his gaze.
  He cannot bear to hear another's praise—
He is half blinded by another's light.

II.

He stabs behind, and in the dark or dusk;
  His swords are *Ifs* and *Buts.* To cloak his
    guile
  He'll sometimes faintly praise, and with a
    smile
Disguise his asafœtida in musk.

III.

Unlike the honest squid, who flings his black
  Full in the face of his pursuing foes,
  He, bland of front, his inky batter throws
On all his rivals—but behind their back.

NATURE.

I.

THE heart of nature soothes the heart of man,
  If with his heart he looks into her eyes.
  A place of leaves, wide air, and sunny skies,
Will soothe him more than even woman can.

II.

We cry, and Nature answers us in time;
  With both hands gives us what we ask and prize;
  A lily pure and pale to glad our eyes,
A spotted toad from out the ooze and slime.

ONE FRIEND.

WHO hath one friend, of straight and loyal mind,
  But one, of all the million swarms of men,
  Is strong, beyond the energy of ten,
Is rich, beyond the level of mankind.

SLIPPING.

THE foot may sooner slip on marble way
  Of royal palace, or in rich man's hall,
  Than on the rough road where the sunbeams fall,
Or cottage paving of the common clay.

LIFE.

A STREAM roars downward to a hidden sea
  That slumbers moonless, starless, without bound,
  Whence comes nor voice, nor form, nor any sound :
The stream is Life, the sea—Eternity.

LOVE IN AGE.

THE hoar and wrinkled trees, long past their prime,
  Hang out, at call of Spring, their green young
    leaves ;
  So when an aged heart Love's call receives,
Hopes, fresh as leaves, rebloom and conquer time.

DAFFODILS.

A SMILE of last year's sun stray'd down the hills,
  And lost its way within yon windy wood;
  Lost through the months of snow, but not for good;
March found it in a clump of daffodils.

UNREST.

WE leave the Good beside us, and uplift
  Wild hands to clutch the Better as our right,
  But somehow miss it in the low dim light.
The Good returns not as a second gift.

Songs.

RED BERRIES OF BRIONY.

RICH was the harvest he vow'd to reap,
  When he planted his germ below;
" Love will give sheaves of red gold to keep,
  And its fruit will be sweet, I know."
      But his golden sheaves
      Are the wrinkled leaves
        By the gusty autumn borne;
      And his fruit, the red berries of briony
        That cling round a wither'd thorn.

" Roses will throw me their blooms," she said,
  " When winter is white on the tree;
Love will bring clusters when leaves are dead—
  The vine's purple clusters to me."
      But her rose-tree stands
      With roseless hands,
        In the cold bleak air forlorn;
      And her clusters are berries of briony
        That cling round a wither'd thorn.

I DREAM'D A DREAM OF AN OLD, OLD LOVE.

I.

I DREAM'D a dream of an old, old love,
    And sweet was that dream to me;
For it brought me the time of my early
      prime,
    And life as it used to be.
We walk'd once more to the village church,
    'Neath the blue of the Sabbath skies;
Down the trysting lane, to the sacred fane,
    With th' light of young love in our eyes;
And again, in the dark pine-woods we stray'd
    Away from the noontide heat,
Where only the thrush broke the silent hush,
    As I lay at my darling's feet.

II.

I dream'd a dream of an old, old love,
    And sweet was that dream of bliss;
For it brought me a hand from the Spirit-land,
    And the touch of a spirit-kiss.
A sense of happiness, pure and strange,
    As a dove on my bosom lay;
With the breath of a wing, with an odour of
      spring,
    My sorrow had pass'd away.
So, I know my old love as an Angel lives,
    Beyond where the pale stars shine,
That she came from above, on a mission of love,
    To bring peace to this soul of mine.

MOO-LE-HU-A.

(A CHINESE SONG.)

—+—

My heart is light, for grief is dead.
The sky is smiling o'er my head,
    Moo-le-hu-a.
I come to thee from stormy seas,
O willow waving in the breeze !
    Moo-le-hu-a.
When three stars shine, wilt thou be mine ?
    Moo-le-hu-a.

The pale moon's scythe of two days old,
I in thine eyebrow's curve behold,
    Moo-le-hu-a.
Thine eyes have far more light within,
Than th' crystal of a mandarin,
    Moo-le-hu-a.
When three stars shine, wilt thou be mine ?
    Moo-le-hu-a.

Thy skin, white wax with rose o'ershed,
Thy budding lips, a crimson thread,
    Moo-le-hu-a—
Long-nailed fingers, night-dark hair;
Thy feet are golden lilies fair,
    Moo-le-hu-a.
When three stars shine, wilt thou be mine?
    Moo-le-hu-a.

Than lotus, fairer thou to me,
Or white flower of the chas-hoo tree,
    Moo-le-hu-a.
When pingtaou blooms, and three stars shine
On evening's brow, I'll make thee mine,
    Moo-le-hu-a.
When three stars shine, thou shalt be mine,
    Moo-le-hu-a.

I.

DISMAL the chamber is, deep in the city,
  Faint is the light in the middle of day ;
Never complaining, but bravely, though weary,
  From morning till evening he labours away.
Father dead, mother dead, left on life's battlefield,
  In the ranks, lonely, to fight for his bread;
Those who once flatter'd look coldly upon him,
  No fortune has he, save his hands and his head.

" *No one to love me ! Oh ! nothing to cling to !*
  Lone as a heron upon a grey stone."

" *Faint not, O heart ! for the Love that is endless*
  Broods o'er the soul that is weary and lone."

II.

Cheerless her window is, wall'd from the sunshine,
  Cheerless the room where the lessons are said.
Often so weary, with lone heart half breaking,
  From morning till evening she works for her bread.

Father dead, mother dead, early a governess,
   Yet was she born to as lofty a lot
As they whose gay voices and light happy laughter
   Ascend to the schoolroom, where she is forgot.

"No one to love me ! Oh ! nothing to cling to !
   High on the mountain, a blossom unknown."

" Faint not, O heart ! for the eyes of the angels
   Rest on the flower that bloometh alone."

III.

'Mid myrtles and roses a fair cottage nestles ;
   Loving the spot, all the sunbeams play there ;
A young mother presses her babe to her bosom,
   And fondly the husband leans over her chair.
Now is she happy, and he is triumphant !
   The big stones are broken that block'd up his way.
They met, both so lonely, loved truly and wedded,
   And twelve months have flown like a sweet summer day.

" Some one to love me ! Oh ! something to cling to !
   No more the lone heron or blossom unknown."

" Rejoice then, O hearts ! for the Love that is endless
   Hath cared for the souls that were weary and lone."

WHY DO I LOVE HER?

I.

NOT for her fortune, her fortune, her fortune,
  Not for the lustre that rests on her name:
      Were her lot lowly,
      Still should I wholly
  Worship her, worship my darling the same!

  Why do I love her?   How can it be?
Because she's herself, just her sweet self to me.

II.

Not only her beauty, her beauty, her beauty,
  Not only the sunshine that lives in her face;
      Something far nearer,
      Sweeter and dearer,
  Binds her to me with its infinite grace.

  Why do I love her?   How can it be?
Because she's herself, just her sweet self to me.

AT THE BEECHEN TREE.

"Oh meet me by the stile," he wrote,
  "The stile beside the beechen tree."
She was the pride o' the country-side,
  He was a sailor home from sea.
      Beside the brook she wends her way,
        The birds sing high! the birds sing low!
      "Now will he come, or will he stay?"
        Her heart says, "Yes;" her heart says,
          "No."

"I did not send an answer back.
  But he should know, I love him well,
For had I told him all he ask'd,
  I should have nothing more to tell."
      So through the wood she wends her way,
        The birds sing high! the birds sing low!
      "Now will he come, or will he stay?"
        Her heart says, "Yes;" her heart says,
          "No."

E

She nears the spot—he is not there—
 " O faithless heart!" she faintly cries.
But he is only hiding near,
 And soon he looks into her eyes.
  Beside the stile he holds her fast,
   The birds sing low, as if to bless.
  " Now give the answer, love, at last."
   Her heart leaps high, her lips say, " Yes."

MY LILY OF THE VALLEY.

WHEN the spring shines in the valley
   Comes the lily leaf to woo,
Calling to his bride, the lily,
   Till she answers, peeping through.
As a maiden sweet, she cometh,
   To her lover lifts her face,
And the tall green leaf enfolds her
   In a tender close embrace.
      So grow to me, as I to thee,
         One, only one, in joy or grief,
        Facing together wind and weather,
        The lily and the leaf.

Now the spring shines in the valley,
   I await thee here alone,
Wait to greet my bride, my lily,
   Wait to call thee all my own.
Come, my darling! come, my flow'ret!
   Lift to me thy radiant face,

And, like lily-leaf, I'll fold thee
To my heart, in close embrace.
    Then grow to me, as I to thee,
        One, truly one, in joy or grief,
    Facing together wind and weather,
        The lily and the leaf.

I WILL NOT TELL.

WHOM do I love ?   I will not say !
    Has he dark eyes,
        Or blue, or grey ?
Lives he so near, or far away ?
      Vain, vain your task,
        In vain you ask
His name—I will not say !

Whom do I love ?   I will not tell !
    His glance wakes Love's
        Enchanting spell.
He lives—in my heart—I know it well.
      Vain, vain your task,
        In vain you ask
His name—I will not tell !

SHE WAITS NO MORE.

THE chestnut buds begin to break,
　　The light stays longer on the lea,
"Oh, surely he will come," she said—
　　　　"Come back to me!"

The poppies burn amid the wheat,
　　The hot winds scorch the weary day.
"Alas! he has not come," said she,
　　　　"From far away."

The days are growing grey and cold,
　　The chestnut leaves are earthward shed—
"He will not come in time," she sighed,
　　　　"Ere I be dead."

The snowflakes fall on carvèd stone,
　　The ship is blown from distant shore—
He comes, her love, he comes—too late!
　　　　She waits no more.

APPLE BLOSSOMS.

— ♦♦ —

HAVE you seen an apple orchard in the spring?
   In the spring?
An English apple orchard in the spring?
  When the spreading trees are hoary
  With their wealth of promise-glory,
  And the mavis pipes his story
   In the spring!

Have you pluck'd the apple blossoms in the spring?
   In the spring?
And caught their subtle odours in the spring?
  Pink buds pouting at the light,
  Crumpled petals baby-white,
  Just to touch them—a delight!
   In the spring!

Have you walk'd beneath the blossoms in the spring?
   In the spring?
Beneath the apple blossoms in the spring?

When the pink cascades are falling,
And the silver brooklets brawling,
And the cuckoo bird is calling,
    In the spring!

Have you seen a merry bridal in the spring?
    In the spring?
In an English apple-county in the spring?
    When the bride and maidens wear
    Apple blossoms in their hair,
    Apple blossoms everywhere
      In the spring!

If you have not, then you know not, in the spring,
    In the spring!
Half the colour, beauty, wonder of the spring.
    No sweet sight can I remember
    Half so precious, half so tender,
    As the apple blossoms render
      In the spring!

THE SONG OF THE FREE.

I.

" OH, sing me a song of your Northern land,"
    Said a Queen to the captive who knelt at her
        feet.
" I would hear of a hero, as true as his brand ;
    Of a maiden all loyal, and fair, and sweet."

II.

" I can sing no song of my Northern land,
    O mighty Queen ! though my life you save ;
For freedom dwells on that wave-wash'd strand,
    And freedom's song is no song for a slave."

III.

" Strike off his chains.   Oh, be free !" she cried ;
    And the fetters fell as her words went forth.
He took his harp with a minstrel's pride,
    And sang of the fame of his distant North.

IV.

Then his spirit rose up, and he shook the strings
 With the strength of a wind that is fierce and
  strong,
And his wild notes soar'd upon burning wings,
 Till dead hearts awoke at his magic song.

V.

For he sang of Hope, and of Liberty,
 Of the banner of Right and of Truth unfurl'd ;
And a great voice grew, like the roar of the sea,
 The voice of an answer from half a world.

VI.

It thrill'd with the promise of good to be,
 Of light that should shine to the uttermost shore—
The minstrel is dust ; but the song of the free
 Rolls onward and upward for evermore !

LIFE.

LIFE is wrought of little things,
Little joys with azure wings,
Little cares with barbéd stings.

Little moments swarm in showers,
Bringing weeds, and bringing flowers,
Dying in the silent hours.

Fall the silent hours away,
Clad in white, and clad in grey,
On the bosom of each day.

Every day its burthen rears,
Sorrow, joyance, pleasure, tears,
Tribute to the hungry years.

And the years sweep out to sea,
Bearing you, and bearing me,
To the wide eternity.

SEA-GULLS.

THE sea has left the shingle,
 The furrow'd sands are dry;
The seven colours mingle
 In the sunset of the sky.

The trailing seaweeds glisten
 On the worn rocks old and grey;
And the small pools seem to listen
 For the sea-voice far away.

The white-wing'd gulls are flying
 Along the water-floor,
Their laughing and their crying
 Break the silence of the shore.

This the burthen of their story,
 Which they pipe between the tides,
"Ours the Sea with all its glory,
 And the little fish besides."

And they call, with wing-commotion,
  To the small pools by the strand,
" When we've done with this our Ocean,
  It will reach you near the land."

MY COTTAGE.

THERE is a cottage somewhere that I love;
  I see it in my dreams at break of day;
I have it not, and yet 'tis mine, above
  The power of human will to take away.

I know it stands green-girded with old trees
  That fence it from the rude borean blasts;
Yet spread their arms to woo each low-voiced
      breeze
  That wantons round it while the summer lasts.

Behind it lifts a tor where heather grows,
  Gold furze, and blossoms loved of fly and bee;
And when, through rifted hills, a strong wind
      blows,
  I sometimes hear the moaning of the sea.

I watch the ships go by to other lands,
   The white sails steal up from the under world ;
Below me sleep the yellow curving sands,
   And leafy coombes wherein the fronds are curl'd.

Its porch——a joy to those who enter in——
   Gives flowery welcome to each guest of mine,
Sweet preface to the human book within,
   In roses, clematis, and eglantine.

It peeps out westward to the setting sun,
   And takes, on tiny spire, his parting rays ;
I watch the star-fires light up one by one,
   The white moon float across the evening haze.

O cottage home ! withdrawn behind the bands
   That hold the Future and its cloudy veil,
When on thy door I lay familiar hands,
   This sombre Now may seem a golden tale.

O yearning human heart ! how fickle ! strange !
   The Now is on me with its crushing load,
Its hard cold lines, its low and narrow range,
   The daily clamber up the broken road.

A MEMORY.

WE were two boys together, he and I;
We met, as men, beneath a neighbour-sky,
In Belgian village.   By its lonely strand,
Its silver sea, by dunes of yellow sand,
Pacing its brick-paved digue or wooden pier,
He talk'd of her.   I lent him friendship's ear.
He was a painter of rare breadth and touch,
A poet, who had thought and suffer'd much.
I loved the man !   I felt 'twas good to be
Awhile with sorrow by that silvery sea.
These words of his, I write from memory.

" Half light of joy, half shadow of regret,
Sweet half pain hoarded in my memory yet,
As gold the miser hoards, who finds at best
His one delight the source of all unrest.

At times," he said, " I live fair days, aud she ⎫
In dream of night or morning reverie, ⎬
Like some loved air, comes back again to me. ⎭

" O voice long lost! O smile! that seem'd so
    true ;
Come back, come back! the tropic past renew.
Vain words !
        For you, I fain would draw aside
The curtains of the silent years that hide
Her face, on which mine eyes have look'd their
    last ;
And bid the night we met—of all the nights
In my spoilt life the fatefulest—rise out
From its deep grave, as it has risen when lights
Are dark within the house, and I alone
Muse like a mourner by a funeral stone.

" O eyes! where dwelt the witchery of power,
Dark eyes and deep that beam'd from out a
    bower
Of lashes curl'd like stamens of a flower.
O hair of night! not flowing light and free
As wintry tresses of the birchen tree,
But serpent-wound and braided royally.

O form ! the beauty of the Greek inbred,
Such gracious curves of brow, and lip, and
    chin,
And stately throat, and fair full breasts wherein
The Love-god's self might rest his drowsy head.

" With magic finger-tips across the keys
Her white hands wander'd, while weird melodies
Crept forth like prison'd sea-nymphs from their
    caves,
Weeping sweet sorrow over moon-lit waves ;
Sighing for sorrow on the lonely seas.
Why sorrow ?   Why should I have heard in these
Unsyllabed revealings of her soul
So much of anguish ?   Was it prophecy,
Foreknowing how the coming days would roll
The bitter tides of pain 'twixt her and me ?

" She sang of woman's faith in olden years,
Of women's love who loved as angels do ;
Her voice was like a star that led me through
A land of love-dreams ; all the air was thrill'd
With nameless raptures, and the wide skies fill'd
With love-light passionate as their own blue.
    She sang of loyalty ; devotion's tears
Stirr'd in her singing, and my glowing heart,
Warm as a boy's who hears of Trojan deeds

And worships Hector, fell before her breath
And worshipp'd her, the singer.   All the creeds
Of olden worlds hold not the counterpart
Of that idolatry that fill'd me then ;
The sweetest madness ever known to men,
Blinder than blind-eyed Fate, and deep as Death.

" The rest is dark," he said—" you know, in part,
How she became my wife ; but in my heart
How she was treasured none can ever know.
She knew it, but too late ! for then the blow
Which shatter'd all my peace had fall'n ; and he,
The striker, at my feet, beside this sea,
Shot down in wrath, lay whining like a cur.
She knew my love, the day I pardon'd her,
And gave her more than half of all I had,
But broke away, for good, and left her—mad !

  . . .

Perhaps I sinn'd in hardness in my pain,
Perhaps I should have brought her home again,—
Our happy home ! "
     A pause—then softly I,
" Where is she now ? "   He answer'd with a sigh :
" The wheel is silent, for the stream is dry,
The dead leaves drift, the green leaf turns to brown,
And on her grave the quiet stars look down."

A BALLAD OF SAINT QUENTIN.

'Twas many a hundred years agone,
   The sun was stooping low—
It shone upon a dying man
   Whose beard was as the snow.

" Oh fetch me here a priest—a priest ;
   Oh ride ye far and fast ;
For he must shrive my guilty soul
   Before the day be past."

So fast they rode by moor and mead,
   Nor drew the bridle-rein
Until they brought a holy friar
   From out Saint Quentin's fane.

" Now sit by me, thou holy man,
   But first the chamber clear,
For I have that to tell to-night
   Which others may not hear—

" And bar the door, thou holy man,
   The casement close with care ;
For I have that to tell to thee
   No wandering wind may bear.

" I was a knight of ancient race,
   Had lands and yellow gold,
My name, good priest ?—nay, ask it not
   Until my tale be told.

" I had a brother, less in age
   Than I by summers three—
I loved a maiden, fair as dawn—
   She loved him more than me.

" I watch'd them in the redd'ning woods,
   I track'd them through the glen ;
One eve, I saw him kiss her lips,
   A madness seized me then.

" And hell awoke within my soul,
   The Fiend hiss'd at my ear—

Ay, cross thyself, thou holy man,
    'Tis a ghastly tale to hear.

" I crouch'd behind a blasted thorn—
    They pass'd me, whispering low ;
Then like a savage thing I sprang,
    And fell'd him at a blow.

" I saw him lying at my feet,
    I stabb'd him as he lay ;—
Nay, stare not so, thou holy friar,
    But tell thy beads and pray.

" There rang a cry, a passionate cry,
    It rang through all the wood !
She knelt beside the dying man,
    And cursed me where I stood.

" An exile have I roam'd since then
    Through many a strange countree ;
But ever, like a slow sleuth-hound,
    Her curse hath follow'd me

" For fifty long, lone, weary years.
    Now would I pardon win ;
Oh lift the cross, thou holy man,
    And shrive me of my sin."

The holy friar, he bows him down,
   And aves mutters three ;
And once, and twice, he tells his beads
   Before a word speaks he.

" Art thou full sure thy brother died ? "
   " Oh ! that too well I know !
I saw the death-glaze in his eyes ;
   I saw his life-blood flow."

' Now, if thou heard'st thy brother lived,
   Would that thy spirit cheer ? "
" Ah, that would be the gladdest word
   That ever I could hear !

" For I would give my castles twain,
   That are beside the sea,
And many a league of rich fat land,
   If such a thing might be.

" Vain, vain ! I know that he is dead,
   For I have seen his sprite
Within the whispering woods at dawn,
   And in the failing light.

" And once it turn'd and seem'd to smile
   As I lay upon my bed ;

Nay—stare not so with thy sad eyes,
　　Thou fill'st my soul with dread."

What ails him now, that holy friar,
　　That he should tremble so?
He kneels beside the aged man,
　　And fast the hot tears flow.

" Look up, look up, good Ethelbert,
　　Thy brother is not dead;
'Tis he who clasps thy hand in his,
　　And kneels beside thy bed."

" Now may Our Ladye pardon thee,
　　If this wonder be not true—
And yet—thy voice—it seems to be
　　The voice of one I knew—

" It draws me back to far-off years;
　　We are two boys again—
There is no blood upon my hand,
　　No devil in my brain.

" And Mervyn woods are broad and green,
　　Oh speak—and let me hear!"
" By every Saint!" said the holy friar,
　　" I am thy brother dear."

The joy that lit the old man's eyes,
　　I ween 'twas good to see.
" Oh ! what of her whose fair young face
　　Did come 'twixt thee and me ? "

" Her body lies in sacred sod,
　　Within a convent wall ;
Her spirit is in Paradise
　　Among the angels all."

.　　　.　　　.　　　.　　　　.

The night went down, the morning broke ;
　　They forced the barréd door,
And there, I trow, was such a sight
　　As scarce was seen before.

With arms about each other's neck,
　　As they were boys in play,
With a look of peace upon each face,
　　In death the brothers lay.

One grave was scoop'd in Quentin's shrine,
　　And many a mass was said,
And bells were toll'd, and tapers burn'd.
　　God rest the quiet dead !

A BALLADE OF MALVERNE CHASE.

(OLD ENGLISH FORM—ABOUT A.D. 1550.)

FROM Malverne Hille she lookt adowne,
　　Her dark eyne glanced athwarte the Chase.
" Why comes not my true Knyght to me,
　　To calle the joye-bloud to my face ?

" Vaine shines the sunne on my brydal morne ;
　　Vaine clang the bells in a measure gaye ;
A shadowe lyes across my hearte,
　　And woe is me ! on my weddinge daye."

The daughter she of a gentyll wighte—
　　Highe Foresteer of the Royale deere—
He had full power of lyfe and lymbe
　　Through alle the Chase, and far and neare.

" Nowe well-adaye ! my hearte is saire !
  My hearte is saire ! " cryed that faire ladye;
" Oh woe is me ! if he come not soon,
  For I shall die in my miserie !

"Oh mickle I feare the fierce Outlawe
  Wille bee to-daye my Love's undoinge ;
For Dunn o' th' Brande wolde give hys righte
      hande
  To mar my Knyght hys wooinge.

" Oh haste awaye ! sith ye love me welle,
  Looke highe and lowe, by brere and yew ;
And I wille give a golden fee
  To alle who succur my Lover true."

They searche them easte, they searche them weste,
  From Coweleighe Cross to Beweleighe Lane,
Or ever they came to the haunted glen,
  They founde the Knyght and a heape of slaine.

By Saint Woolstann ! sin' the worlde beganne
  Was never, I wis, such a sight to see !
The deade Knyght sat hym against a thorne,
  And the Outlawes bore hym companie.

For two laye starke at hys lefte hande,
    As deade were they as a coffin boarde;
And eke two more upon hys righte,
    Pierced throughe and throughe with hys trustye
        sworde.

And he, the Chief, the fierce Outlawe,
    Hys face as wan as a wyndinge-sheete,
Dark Dunn o' th' Brande, without hys righte hande,
    Laye colde and stille at the Knyght hys feet.

Five foes to one, they on hym felle,
    Five swordes to one throughe halfe the night;
Though five to one, they were overcome,
    Five foes laye deade in the morninge light.

" Nowe take ye boughen from the tree,
    Nowe make a bedde of the leavis greene;
And we wille beare to holy grounde
    The bravest Knyght was ever seene."

They wende them slowlye throughe the woode,
    They chaunte a dirge so weird and shrille,
She hearde it on the bittere winde,
    And alle her bloud ranne colde and chille.

With water from the holy-welle,
    With many a signe of the sacred tree,

They washed the brave deade Knyght hys woundes,
   And brought hym to the Pryourie.

In Jesu Chapelle, ryche and dimme,
   They layed hym, dresst in Death's wycht gowne,
Where from each window's pictured pane,
   Hys deare Lorde Master lookt adowne.

" Ah woe is me ! " cryes the sadde Ladye,
   " My sweete deade Love, he waites hys bride,
This night it is our brydal night,
   And I wille laye me by hys side."

In purfled amice dight was she,
   Alle emerants and pearles wycht,
With marriage flouris round her heade,
   It was, I wis, a pityous sight !

Like wroughten marble was her face,
   So stedfaste sette in her despaire ;
Yet wrung she not her small wycht handes,
   Nor broke one threade of her raven haire.

She moved alonge with firm slowe step,
   With wide eyne fixt, as she hadde seene
A wycht star on a far-off hille,
   And heeded not what laye atween.

So gained she to the Pryourie,
 Withouten pause, withouten dreade,
Bent over, kist her loved Lord's face,
 Then laide her by her noble deade.

Her maides, a group of flouris pale,
 Worne by the raine of bittere griefe,
Before the Holy Altar kneel,
 And weepinge, praye for her reliefe.

The night weares downe and silence falls,
 Nowe lifted by a sobb of woe,
And nowe, by chaunte of olden hymne,
 And sisters' voices softe and lowe.

Eftsoons the drearye morninge breakes,
 The wide worlde wakes to joye or paine ;
Her maides up from their knees do rise,
 But she will never wake againe.

Her face is as the lilye wycht,
 Her hande is colde as any stone ;
For grief she died on her weddinge night.
 Sure sadder tale was never knowne !

By the Danube.

Sonnet.

ATTILA.

THE kingdoms trembled, Princes shook with fear,
   Imperial Rome flung forth a cry of woe,
   When Attila's fierce star's ensanguined glow
Had lit, with awful glare, a hemisphere.
A prodigy of valour! 'neath his spear,
   The startled lions of the West crouch'd low;
   Victorious fortune scatter'd every foe,
And bade the glory of the Huns appear.

But who shall track high Heaven's fateful thread?
   A world in arms had fail'd, with war unfurl'd,
To strike the blow that in her bridal bed
   The fair Idolca struck.   Her dagger hurl'd
From life and strife, ere age had bow'd his head,
   The "Scourge of God," the "Terror of the World."

G

KING STEPHEN'S CROWN.

A.D. 1000.

— —•• — —

NIGHT moonless sank on Estergom,
    On Palace and on town;
But lovingly, like spirit-eyes,
    The diamond-stars look'd down.
The river Gran swept by to join
    Her Danube's seaward race ;
A willing bride, to throw herself
    Into his wild embrace.
The winds were hush'd, the stately trees
    Had sway'd themselves to sleep ;
And Magyar chief, Sclavonian, Jew,
The Christian priest, the Scythian too,
    Lay wrapp'd in slumber deep.
But here and there, among the poor,
    Gaunt hunger broke the rest ;

The squalid babe, with piteous moan,
  Forsook the famish'd breast;
And haggard men turn'd restlessly,
  And women, worn with care,
Awoke from dreams of eager feast
  And groan'd in their despair;
For flocks were few, and fields lay waste,
  And spades were red with rust,
And many a sturdy peasant arm
  Lay stricken in the dust;
Religious war had curs'd the land,
  And brothers drew the sword,
And some for Scythian gods had fought,
  And some for Christ the Lord.

The Palace stands out grim and dark
  Upon its rocky height;
But, from the middle turret gleams
  A faint yet steady light.
'Tis from the chamber of the King,
  King Stephen, good and wise,
For him, the gentle dews of sleep
  Fall not on weary eyes;
Care sits upon his lofty brow,
  A nation's wearing care;
A nation's sorrow in each line
  So deeply furrow'd there.

To frame good laws and wise decrees,
    To foster truth and right ;
To heal his country's bleeding wounds,
    He toils into the night.
For this, his lonely lamp is lit,
    His sagest schemes are plann'd ;
To make Hungaria strong and free,
    A great, a Christian land.

His taper throws a soften'd light
    Within that vaulted room ;
It falls on battle-dinted shield,
    On sword and helmet's plume,
It creeps along the storied walls,
    And clasps, with ghostly grace,
The arms uncouth of ancient war,
    The trophies of the chase ;
It rests on spoils of glorious art
    Wrought in old Rome or Greece,
And on a fair white marble cross,
    The Christian's sign of peace.
Before that cross the Priest-King kneels, ·
    In prayer he seeks relief,
Outpouring in the gloom of night
    The torrent of his grief.

"How long, O Lord! shall civil strife
    Among my people dwell?
How long, O Lord! shall Pagan gloom
    Against Thy light rebel?
Oh heal the land—a brother's brand
    Now seeks a brother's life;
Oh heal the land—the husband's hand
    Is raised against the wife;
Oh heal the land—our flocks are few,
    Thy poor are hardly fed;
Oh heal the land—our fields are bare,
    Thy children cry for bread.
Arise! and break the Pagan chains,
    And set the prisoners free;
'Arise! with healing in Thy wings,'
    And draw all men to Thee."

King Stephen rose, he paced the room;
    High-heap'd before him spread
A waste of gold and precious gems;
    Then, musingly, he said—
"O gold, red gold, a gift, a curse,
    A blessing, used aright,
A curse, if used for selfish ends,
    Thou break'st my sleep to-night!

I give thee to a craftsman's hand,
　　Well-skill'd, of fair renown,
To make, adorn'd with these rich gems,
　　My Coronation Crown ;
While all around my Palace gates,
　　With nought to purchase bread,
This scroll declares —the poor abound,
　　Unclothed, unwarm'd, unfed.
Now, by the Rood ! for brighter days
　　My crown shall wait—full sure
Its gold would scorch my brow and brain
　　If taken from the poor.
O gold, red gold, a gift, a curse,
　　A blessing, used aright,
A curse, if used for selfish ends,
　　Thou break'st my sleep to-night."

The King drew on an ample cloak ;
　　He took his golden store ;
Stepp'd through his sleeping guards, unseen,
　　And pass'd the outer door.
He gain'd the town ; he sought the poor,
　　The sick, infirm, and old ;
And at each door the good King laid
　　A piece of shining gold.

The hours flew by, but onward still,
  Still on the monarch went;
A faint flush graced the eastern sky ;
  The golden store was spent.
Full many a heart grew glad next day,
  And each the wonder told,
How a good Angel had come down
  And strew'd the town with gold.

A year pass'd by—a wondrous crown,
  With sapphire lights inlaid,
To Stephen came. Rome's mighty Pope
  The splendid offering made.
A wondrous crown of beaten gold,
  With many a diamond spark
Outlooking from each subtle sphere,
  Like stars from out the dark.
And twelve enamels of the Saints
  And holy men of eld,
Refulgent with the tints of noon,
  In golden circlets held ;
And in the centre, Christ the Lord
  With long dishevell'd curls,
Framed fair in amethystine rays
  And the sheeny light of pearls.

And from the circle's sparkling rim
    Nine golden chains hung down;
While mystic trefoils, diamond-lit,
    Adorn'd King Stephen's crown.

Right royally the monarch wore
    That crown through changeful years :
But fairer than its fairest gem
    His blameless life appears.
He law from out disorder drew,
    And with an arm of might
Drove Wrong to cower in its den
    Abash'd before the Right;
Broke up the Pagan hordes, and ere
    He pass'd to brighter day,
Beheld the Christian verities
    Hold universal sway.
From Tatra's crags to Duna's banks,
    And Thesis' watery hem,
Was felt the firm wise rule of him
    Who wore that diadem.
At length, full flush'd with golden years,
    True love, and reverence wide,
He laid, amid a people's tears,
    His earthly rule aside.
But a better crown awaited him,
    A beam of his Master's love ;

A glory round his sainted brow,
   In the Heavenly Courts above.

Though dead and gone, in smiles, in tears,
His lamp still shines through misty years,
   Still greets us from afar.
Undimm'd by time, unquench'd by might,
The Magyar turns to bless its light,
   His country's morning-star !

WARRIOR, RISE!

THE Lion has bounded from his lair;
He tosses his mane to the startled air;
The voice of his thunder stretches wide;
The shepherd turns pale on the mountain-side.
   Warrior, rise! thy weapon draw,
    Save the Lamb from the Lion's paw.

The Eagle has soar'd above his nest;
The towering crags beneath him rest;
He watches, fierce-eyed, each fleecy troop,
And poises his wings for the fatal swoop.
   Warrior, rise! thy weapon draw,
    Save the Lamb from the Eagle's claw.

The foeman has cross'd the guardian pass ;
His spears, as the forest, make night on the grass ;
As clouds are his banners ; his hands are red ;
The green earth trembles beneath his tread.
　　Warrior, warrior ! draw thy brand,
　　Strike for Home and Fatherland !

THE BLACK PLUME.

"On the wide plains of Pannonia,
   Cymbals clash, and trumpets blare,
In the sacred strife for freedom,
   Calling me to do and dare.
Must I leave thee ? near one—dear one !
   Answer, wife ! " Then answer'd she—
" Take the sword thy fathers fought with.
   Strike for Hungary and for me."
         'Neath the old linden-tree
         Sits the wife dreamily ;
         Wither'd leaves silently
            Fall at her feet.

Yonder move the Austrian masses ;
   Death stands facing every eye ;
But their hearts refuse to falter,
   They will conquer or will die.

" Magyars ! " cries their leader gaily—
  " White hands this good falchion gave ;
For our loved ones, follow swiftly
    Where you see my black plume wave."
        'Neath the old linden-tree
        Sits the wife dreamily ;
        Wither'd leaves sighingly
          Fall at her feet.

Din of drums and bray of bugles,
  Martial-music's rousing swell,
Roll of muskets, boom of cannon,
  Whiz of shot and bursting shell,
War-horse snorting, sabres clashing,
  Cries of men who scorn to yield,
Wail of wounded, groans of dying,
  Rise up from the battlefield.
        'Neath the old linden-tree
        Sits the wife dreamily;
        Wither'd leaves sighingly
          Fall at her feet.

Brute-force, with its surging thousands,
  Rears aloft its hydra-head,
Pouring from its deadly trenches—
  Pouring fiery showers of lead.

'Mid the blue smoke waves a black plume,
    Where the bellowing cannon roar,
Where the bullets fall as hailstones,
    And the sod is wet with gore.
            'Neath the old linden-tree
            Sits the wife dreamily;
            Wither'd leaves sighingly
                Fall at her feet.

Onward sweeps the tide of conflict
    In its red resistless course;
Fierce as ocean lash'd to fury,
    Breaking with a mighty force;
But as rock against the waters
    Stand the patriot few to-day.
Marvel not! they fight for country,
    Home, and freedom, in the fray.
            'Neath the old linden-tree
            Sits the wife dreamily;
            Wither'd leaves sighingly
                Fall at her feet.

" Yonder! past their bristling cannon,
    Yonder, brothers, must we go;
Years of wrong, one hour of vengeance—
    Let us grapple with the foe!"

Up the steep he bears the colours—
  Talpra vitez ! ours the day !
Hark ! their *elgin* smites the Heavens,
  And the grim foe melts away.
      'Neath the old linden-tree
      Sits the wife dreamily ;
      Wither'd leaves sighingly
        Fall at her feet.

As the driftwood of the forest
  When the whirlwind rushes through,
When the boughs are bare in winter,
  Fled the many from the few ;
Left their guns, and left their trenches,
  Left their wounded, and their slain,
Left their colours, and their comrades,
  On the cumber'd battle-plain.
      'Neath the old linden-tree,
      Sits the wife dreamily ;
      Wither'd leaves sighingly
        Fall at her feet.

Where the mound of death was deepest,
  Lay the black plume, fleck'd with blood ;
Lay their hero, gash'd and gory,
  Stiffen'd in a crimson'd flood.

But a look of joy and triumph
   Graced his features calm and proud,
And the colours that he carried
   Cover'd him as with a shroud.
       'Neath the old linden-tree
       Sits the wife dreamily,
       Wither'd leaves sighingly,
         Fall at her feet.

Now the sky is black and murky,
   And the wind wails o'er the plain,
Soft and mournful, nature's sorrow
   For the orphans and the slain ;
And they bury him, their darling!
   Stout of heart, the true and tried,
On the red field where he conquer'd
   In his glory and his pride.
       Still, 'neath the linden-tree
       Sits the wife dreamily,
       Wither'd leaves sighingly,
       Moaningly, dyingly,
         Fall at her feet.

SHADOWS.

A Tiszian maiden,
Laughter-laden,
Leant beside a garden gate ;
Musing, smiling,
Self-beguiling,
Thinking on her absent mate.

A Chikosh, youthful,
Honest, truthful,
Was that favour'd absent mate ;
Came he slyly,
Look'd round shyly,
Then stood bashful near the gate.

He was gallant,
Brave and gallant,
Stout of heart, and stout of limb ;

H

But, through Cupid
He look'd stupid;
She look'd furtively at him.

Lost in wonder,
Quite asunder,
Stood he from that dark-eyed maid.
" Why so slyly
Come you nigh me?
You're not wanted, sir," she said.

" See—our shadows,
Our *two* shadows,
Painted by the slanting sun.
Madre might see,
So might Padre—
Would the shadows could be *one*!

" If, when keeping
Watch, and peeping,
Madre see *one* shadow lie,
From her curtain,
She'll feel certain
I'm alone, and you're not by."

Still in wonder,
Still asunder,
Stood he from that Tiszian maid;
Eyes paid duty
To her beauty,
But to near—he seem'd afraid.

Then she pouted,
Then she flouted,
Then she said her finger pain'd—
He stood sighing,
Vainly trying
Some sweet speech which he had feign'd.

From her bright eyes
Dancing light flies,
Crowds his pulses with a glow.
Each grows dearer,
Shadows nearer
Tremble as the moments go.

Feelings thronging,
Yearning, longing,
Their hands meet—they can't tell how;
Coldness dies off,
Shyness flies off,
Tongue-tied he no longer now.

And she nestles,
To him nestles,
Glowing, willing to be prest;
While his strong arms
Fold her young charms
To his bunda-cover'd breast.

And he prays her,
Fondly prays her,
To become his own—his wife;
Two no longer,
Loving stronger,
One in heart, and one in life.

She replying,
Not denying,
" See, my heart, the sinking sun
On the pad throws
Not *two* shadows,
Love has made our shadows *one.*"

BY THE WATCH-FIRE.

"COME, heap more wood upon the fire,
  And bid the red wine flow;
The night we'll give to song and mirth,
  The morrow to the foe!
The Turkish hosts, by Duna's side,
  In swarthy myriads lie,
Thick as the falling forest leaves,
  When autumn winds are high;
Thick as the locusts on the march,
  When the springing corn is green,
The wingèd thieves spread right and left,
  And nothing lives between.
They come, as in the days of old,
  When Bela was our King,
The Mongul monsters came, and stung
  Our sires with deadly sting.

They come, as then, to sack, to burn,
   To make a blacken'd track
Of this, our own, our sunny land—
   Shall we not drive them back ?
Ay, Brothers ! like a storm we'll rise
   And sweep them from the sod ;
For we shall strike for hearth and home,
   For country, and for God !
Then heap more wood upon the fire,
   And bid the red wine flow ;
The night we'll give to song and mirth,
   The morrow to the foe."

Thus spake a Hunnish warrior eld
   (Brave Bator was he hight),
As round the watch-fire group'd his band,
   The eve before the fight.
Then rising to his feet, he said—
   While eyes were bent on him—
" Fill, fill this mighty cup with wine ;
   Ay, fill it to the brim—
And here's a pledge, and here's a name,
   As the goblet passes round,
Shall speed the life-blood to your heart,
   And make your pulses bound.
The Magyar loves the tented field,
   The war-horse, and the lance,

The merry trill of gipsy song,
 The twinkle of the dance,
The bright eyes of a maiden brown,
 The rich wine, as it glows,
But deeper still—a crownèd King
 To lead him on his foes!
And since great Arpad taught us war,
 Was never such a knight
In hall, or camp, in love, or strife,
 As I will name to-night.
Drink to our strong and dauntless King,
 Matthias, firm and free !
God give him health ! God give him wealth !
 To-morrow—victory !
Then heap more wood upon the fire,
 And bid the red wine flow ;
The night we'll give to song and mirth,
 The morrow to the foe ! "

ILLONA.

I.

Oh! I have lost Illona,
My love with the shining hair,
And night-dark eyes,
So deep and wise,
And brow divinely fair.
I have sought her in the meadows,
And 'neath the rowan-tree,
Where, in the glow
Of a young moon's bow,
She gave her heart to me.
Say—have you seen Illona?
My wild wood-flower, Illona?
Her voice is sweet,
Her foot is fleet,
Dark-eyed Illona!

II.

I have wander'd by the river,
  By the music-making rills ;
    I have stray'd beside
    The waters wide,
  I have rambled o'er the hills ;
But ah ! I cannot find her,
  I fear that she is dead,
    And I would rest
    On her cold breast
This weary, wilder'd head.
    Soon I shall die, Illona,
    My goddess-brow'd Illona ;
      The cut branch weeps,
      The dead branch sleeps,
      Dark-eyed Illona.

III.

Last night, last night I saw her
  All in a winding sheet ;
    She seem'd to glide
    O'er Duna's tide
With moonbeams at her feet.
She raised a weird wan finger,
  And bent her eyes on me,

And whisper'd low,
So faint and low,
Oh come ! Oh come to me !
I come, I come, Illona !
The long light breaks, Illona
In spirit-land,
I touch thy hand,
Dark-eyed Illona !

BATTHYÁNYI.

At night in my dreams thou art with me;
    I gaze on thy soul-beaming face;
I drink thy sweet breath, and I fold thee
    So long in a tender embrace.

Our little one nestles beside thee,
    Asleep in its ivory nest—
Forgotten my chains and my anguish;
    I pillow my head on thy breast.

Thy lips breathe my name in a murmur;
    Thy white hand clasps mine, as of old;
I wake—all my fetters are clanking,
    And the wind through my dungeon blows cold.

THE BRIDGE OF STRAUBING.

In one of the three chapels planted round the churchyard of St. Peter's Church, outside of the walls of the town of Straubing, a tombstone is pointed out as that which covers the grave of the unfortunate Agnes Bernauer. Though the daughter of a bumble citizen of Augsberg, this fair damsel by her beauty and virtue gained the heart of Albert, son of Duke Ernest of Bavaria. Albert was privately married to her, but, unfortunately for the happiness of the youthful couple, their secret reached the ears of the Duke, who had planned for his son a more exalted match. The father, taking advantage of his son's absence, caused Agnes to be seized, condemned to death upon false accusations, and cast from the Bridge of Straubing into the Danube.

Having succeeded in freeing herself from her bonds, the poor victim, shrieking for help and mercy, endeavoured to reach the bank, and had nearly effected a landing, when a miscreant caught her by her long hair, and dragging her back into the stream, held her under water until the tragedy was completed.

The fury and despair of Albert on hearing of her shameful death were boundless. He fled, and in open rebellion joined the army of Louis the Bearded, his father's bitterest foe, and with him invaded his native land to take vengeance on the murderers of his bride.

The chronicler adds that this deadly and unnatural feud lasted for many years.

THE BRIDGE OF STRAUBING.

"HE said, 'I will return ere dark;'
   He told me not to fear:
The dark has come, the stars are out,
   But Albert is not here.
Behind the open lattice, where
   We twain have sat, I wait,
That I may rush to meet him, when
   His hand is on the gate.
How fair the days have dawn'd for me
   Since that sweet Easter-tide,
When love amidst its flowers came
   And claim'd me as a bride!

"O sweet half-year of cloudless skies!
   O fields and happy flowers!
O sunny morns! O golden nights!
   O laughter-laden hours!

A step—he comes!　Alas! 'tis gone—
　　It passes by the gate;
Some weary peasant trudging home—
　　Lie still, poor heart, and wait!

" How weirdly loom the poplars tall!
　　The passion-flowers o'erhead
Are trembling, yet I feel no wind;
　　And now a bloom falls dead.
The farthest darkness seems to take
　　Strange shapes that cheat the eye;
The very silence throbs with sounds—
　　I listen, and they die.
He said, ' I will return ere dark ; '
　　He told me not to fear.
The dark has come, the stars are out,
　　But Albert is not here.

' Why comes he not ?　I know he seeks
　　The Duke, his haughty sire,
Duke Ernest, stern, they say, and proud,
　　Of fierce and vengeful ire ;
And he will tell of all our love,
　　How he woo'd and won his bride,
And I shall ride in cloth-of-gold,
　　A lady by his side ;

For ere he left he kiss'd me thrice,
    And press'd me to his heart—
'Sweet Agnes, till our days be done
    No power shall make us part;
And by my knightly faith I swear
    That thou shalt take thy stand
Before the world, my wedded wife,
    The proudest in the land!'
These were his words, his last loved words—
    Why is my heart not light?
Why sits a fear of coming woe
    Upon my soul to-night?
The air seems stirr'd with viewless wings,
    My senses creep with dread;
Is it the pulsing of my heart,
    Or did I hear his tread?
He said 'I will return ere dark;'
    He told me not to fear:
The dark has come, the moon is up,
    But Albert is not here.

"He comes! he comes! my own! my life!
    Fly, laggard love, be fleet!
But hark! What means this sound of tongues,
    This noise of many feet?
Why comes he not alone to-night?"
    But ere her words had died,

Three armèd men of savage mien
    Rush'd in and seized the bride.
" Unhand me !—Hold ! what want you here ?
    Can it be gold you seek ? "
Amazed at such rare loveliness,
    Those rough men could not speak,
But each fell back, and silent gazed
    On face and ruffled brow ;—
Duke Ernest, Lord of all the land,
    Enters the chamber now.
" Oh where is Albert ?—speak, my Lord,—
    My Albert, brave and true ? "
" Peace," said the Duke, " that knight is lost
    For evermore to you."
" Nay, nay, my Lord, recall your words,
    Pray God it may not be !
For I am all the world to him,
    And he is all to me."

She sank down in a suppliant curve,
    So innocent, so sweet ;
She look'd up in his frowning face,
    She clung about his feet :
" You will not part us, gentle Duke,
    No ! no ! 'twere death in life !
He is my husband, leal and true,
    And I am his true wife."

Duke Ernest forth a casket drew,
Which holy relics hid from view,
   And said, " Know I full sure
That thou art not Lord Albert's wife ;
Now swear on these for very life
   He is thy paramour.
Nay, start not ! frown not ! thou canst make
   Of me a foe or friend ;
Deny this rite, this marriage-bond,
   So shall mischances end ;
These men will bear thee far away
   Safe to a distant land,
With dainty robes, and costly gems,
   And gold at thy command ;
The fragrant dish, the silken couch,
   The red juice of the vine,
And all that makes life full of life,
   I promise shall be thine.
Upon these sacred relics swear
   Thou art not wedded wife ;
But dare refuse—this scroll condemns :
   To-night I take thy life."

She started proudly to her feet,
   She spake with flashing eye,
" That I am Albert's wedded wife
   I never will deny.

1

Though life to me is dear and sweet,
    And death a gloomy shore,
Though I love life so well," she said,
    " I love my honour more."

The old knight clench'd his mailèd hand,
    He stamp'd his foot in scorn :
" Prat'st thou of honour thus, forsooth ?
    Thou, a poor peasant born ?
Thou art a witch ; by hellish arts
    Hast thou beguiled my son."
" Now, by the Holy Cross," said she,
    " No witch-deed have I done ;
He sought me for my own poor self,
    Though high in rank was he
He woo'd and won my virgin heart,
    And then he wedded me.
Yes, wedded me ! in Holy Church
    Was breathed the mystic vow ;
And though I was a peasant born,
    I am his equal now ! "

A coarse curse, like an adder, hiss'd
    From fierce lips parch'd and white :
" The eagle mates not with the crow ;
    The crow shall die to-night."
He gave a sign his creatures knew ;
    Obeying it full soon,

They drag her, fair as sculptured saint,
    Beneath the peering moon.
Along the dusty road they trail
    Her dark dishevell'd hair—
Would that brave Albert, sword in hand,
    Could meet those ruffians there !
They reach old Straubing's fatal bridge—
    Ah ! deed of dire disgrace—
The sad moon hides behind a cloud
    Her pale affrighted face :
The Danube roars, the deep wind wails,
    The night-birds loudly scream ;
One long, lorn, terror-laden cry—
    They've thrown her in the stream.

The clouds clear off, and silvery beams
    A halo round her throw,
Illume each stone upon the bridge,
    Each broken wave below.
See ! see ! she breasts the angry flood,
    She struggles with the tide,
She nears the bank—by all the Saints
    She'll reach the further side !

Oh haste thee ! haste thee, gallant knight !
    And give a helping hand ;

Yea! leap into the swollen stream,
　　And draw her safe to land.
He grasps her flowing hair—and now—
　　O God! that there should be
In all the world so black a heart,
　　So base a wretch as he!
He holds her head *beneath* the surge—
　　A struggle—all is o'er—
And she, so lovely and so true,
　　Is still for evermore.

A great light on the waters fell,
　　Sweet whispers floated by,
And melting strains of far-off song
　　Were wafted from the sky;
And then a wreath of mist arose
　　From the spot where Agnes sank;
Duke Ernest saw it seek the stars,
　　Then, shuddering, left the bank.

Fair Agnes—many a bard has sung
　　Her beauty and her bale,
And many a fair Bavarian maid
　　Has wept to hear her tale;
Wept too for Albert, hapless knight,
　　Who, hastening to her side,

Met on the bridge her murder'd corse,
   Just rescued from the tide.
He took her cold, cold hand in his,
   And there with passionate breath
He swore, upon her silent heart,
   He would avenge her death.

.   .   .   .

Long years have past, in Straubing town,
   By Danube's turbid wave;
They still show, near its ancient church,
   Her venerated grave.
And History tells how civil war
   Raged like a roaring flood;
How son 'gainst sire waged deadly strife,
   And dyed the land with blood;
And how the old Duke mourn'd his heir,
   As the ghastly years went by,
While in his lurid soul was nursed
   The worm that would not die.

HARALD.

(FROM THE GERMAN OF UHLAND.)

——✦——

BEFORE his glittering retinue
    Rides Harald, brave and good,
Rides with his band, all moonbeam lit,
    Into the haunted wood.

They bear aloft the banner won
    In field of fiercest fight;
Their songs of war and victory
    Startle the solemn night.

But ah ! what stirs in bush and tree,
    Sails on each bright moonbeam,
Drops from the violet-tinted clouds,
    Springs from the ferny stream ?

Fair forms that 'mid the horsemen glide,
    Strewing fresh flowers around,
While sweet songs through the leafy wood
    Enchantingly resound.

They weave white arms round stalwart necks,
    Warming each mailèd breast ;
Their kisses fall on bearded mouths
    So tenderly carest.

They draw, then fling the swords away,
    With wiles that still increase ;
They lure the warriors from their steeds,
    And rob them of their peace.

They are the bright elves of the wood,
    A semi-human band—
Spellbound, each warrior leaves his lord,
    And goes to faery-land.

But he, Sir Harald, brave and free,
    All clad in armour tried,
Still holds his good sword in his hand,
    And will not turn aside.

His knights, his squires have gone—there lie
    Their swords and bucklers good ;

Each proud steed, from his master freed,
    Flies wild within the wood.

Sad, sorrow-laden, 'mid dim trees
    That flung weird arms on high,
He rode, and reach'd where rugged rocks
    Were piled against the sky.

And water, crystalline and cool,
    From out the grey rocks burst;
Sir Harald sprang down from his horse,
    For he was sore athirst.

He scarce had quench'd his thirst, and laid
    His helmet on the bank,
When all the vigour of his limbs
    Forsook him, and he sank—

He sank upon the rock.   The stream
    In awful splendour leapt;
The Lethe draught benumb'd his soul,
    He nodded, and he slept.

And still he slumbers, head on breast,
    Though centuries have flown:
His grey beard waves, his armour shakes
    Upon the rugged stone.

When lightnings flash, and thunders roll,
    And storms roar through the trees,
The peasant hears him draw his sword,
    And clank it in the breeze.

FROM THE GERMAN OF HEINE.

I LOOK on thee, sweet floweret,
   So fresh, and pure, and fair;
While on my heart creeps slowly
   The shadow of a care.

I'd lay my hands devoutly
   Upon thy golden hair;
And pray God keep thee ever,
   As fresh, and pure, and fair.

Song.

HOME.

(FROM THE GERMAN.)

ASK'D I the weary wanderer,
  "Whence comest thou?"
    "Home, Home, *from* Home.'
He sigh'd, with sadden'd brow.

Ask'd I then the peasant boy,
  "Whither thy way?"
    "Home, Home, *my* Home!"
He cried in accents gay.

Ask'd I next a smiling one,
  "Where dwells delight?"
    "Home, Home, *at* Home!"
Said he, with glances bright.

Ask'st thou me why oft I sigh ?
Why restless roam ?—
Home, Home, *no* Home,
I have no more a Home !

Song.

GUTEN MORGEN.

Guten Morgen! Drowsy flowers,
  On your eyelids hangs the dew;
Waken, waken, sleepy flowers,
  I have come to talk to you.
Send your sweet breaths o'er the lea,
     O'er the lea,
To a maiden fair to see,
     Fair to see,
  And I'll greet you heartily,
    Guten Morgen! Guten Morgen!
I will greet you tenderly,
     Guten Morgen!

Guten Morgen! Golden sunbeam,
  Sailing on the morning air,

Will you take a message, sunbeam,
    To a maiden passing fair ?
Gild the couch where sleepeth she,
    Where sleepeth she,
Kiss her cheek, and say from me,
    Say from me,
    That I greet her heartily,
      Guten Morgen ! Guten Morgen !
    That I love her tenderly,
      Guten Morgen !

Miscellaneous.

THE BEDFORDSHIRE PLAIT GIRL.

Before a rustic cottage door,
    And sitting in the sun,
I saw a girl some eight years old,
    And another little one.

Each left arm held a hoop of plait
    Fast growing to a score;
For quickly moved their fingers small
    As I drew near the door.

"Well done! my tiny folks," said I;
    Then, to the elder maid,
"Is this your little sister here,
    So busy at her trade?"

K

" Yes, sir," she said, and from her mouth
    Another straw she took;
" An' that's my brother Billy there,
    'A plattin' by the brook."

" Do others plait as young as you ? "
    " Why, yes, in course they do !
There's Billy, he are less than she,
    An' Billy, he plaits too."

" You love a game, I'm sure," said I,
    " When plaiting task is o'er."
" Yes, mother lets us play sometimes,
    When we 'ave done our score."

" Of course you go to school," I said;
    She shook her sunny head;
" Oh please sir, we don't go to school,
    We 'as to earn our bread."

" You cannot read ? "   " No sir, not yet;
    But Jane Smith can, I'm told;
And as for I, I means to try—
    " That is, when I are old."

" What can you earn ?   You cannot say;
    Come, try and give a guess."

" Well, sometimes eight'n pence a week,
 But sometimes I earns less.

" When father had the fever, sir,
 We little money got ;
But a lady came and buy'd my plait,
 An' then I earn'd a lot !

" But mother splits the straws for me,
 An' she does more nor that ;
She clips the ends, an' mills it too,
 Afore she sells the plait.

" An' then she takes all what we've made,
 An' though it rains or snows,
To sell it all, on market-days,
 To Dunstable she goes.

" But mother says that, by-and-by,
 If I makes 'aste an' grows,
As I shall go to Luton, sir,
 Where everybody sews !

" I do so long for that to come,
 I are so proud to grow ;
They don't do plait at Luton, sir,
 They only has to sew ! "

Hard-working little lass ! thought I,
    Thou'st taught, in childish speech,
How much akin are human aims,
    Link'd closely each to each.

Some distant Luton we desire,
    Some duty we despise ;
We plan, we strive, we hope, until
    The long sleep shuts our eyes.

MEMORY PICTURES.

UPON the mirror-surface of the mind
The Beautiful imprints itself, in shades
And colours of its own, and thenceforth lives,
Through passing days and all the weighted years,
A precious picture of the memory.
    Not all of Beauty seen by us so lives,
But that which flashing on the inward sight
Reveals its sense to ours and stays with us,
Grows part of us and makes us rich, becomes
What he, "the sweet dead singer," call'd "a joy
For ever."
                I, with eyelids closed, behold
At times, imperfectly, as if a mist
Had drawn itself across, at times most clear,
These dear presentments of the past.

The scene,
The hour, I first confronted face to face
The unutterable wonder of the sea;
The birth of day, when snowy mountain peaks
Were drench'd with glory by the climbing sun;
A rose-clad cottage, sloping into shade
Of apple boughs; a green path through a wood,
With burning gold of broom on either hand;
Night on an English river, meadows dark,
Whose willows, drooping low with sorrowing
    leaves,
At sound of sweet sad music trembling near,
Wept tears of moonlight in the sleeping stream.
Amid such pictures of my buried days,
Familiar as the face of long-loved friend,
There comes to me at times, when lights are low,
And silence sits beside me in the house,
One scene, of all most vividly impress'd,
When tender chords gave Heavenly symphonies,
And unlock'd hearts closed not again for joy.

Ah! who hath not in memory's secret cell,
Enshrined 'mid holy things, fresh, truthful, pure,
The tender reflex of a human face?
Ah! I have one, a winsome, speaking face,
A gentle woman's trusting, loving face.
I see it now, as when, a passionate boy,

In village school—extemporised a church—
I saw it first.   The forms so closely placed,
The narrow room—seat opposite to seat—
The sermon long, and logical, and dry ;
And yet regretfully I heard it close,
For holy music murmur'd in my ear,
And, 'neath a winter cloak, my young heart saw
The folded whiteness of an Angel's wings,
And found a Heaven in those sea-grey eyes.

Belovèd face ! I greet thee yet again ;
Age cannot dim thy beauty, cankering care
Can 'grave no furrows on thy lovely brow ;
No silver rivulets can ever run
Adown the masses of thy golden hair ;
The bloom upon thy cheek can never fade,
The redness of thy lips, the trembling light
Of those sweet eyes can never pass away.
As long as reason sits upon its throne,
As long as these poor pulses beat, so long,
Fair picture of my youth, wilt thou endure.

CONCERNING LOVE.

You know not what you ask—to bid me tell,
In words, the wonder of the Love-god's spell.
'Tis vain, dear Heart!   I'd need Apollo's lyre
To breathe the love-thoughts which your eyes
　　inspire.
Those thoughts are finer than the spider's wire;
And they are warmer than the mountain's fire;
And deeper than the ocean's hidden wells;
And fairer than his coral caves and shells,
His sea-nymphs, running fingers through their
　　curls,
In crystal caverns lit with sheeny pearls.
Ah, love! and wider than the southern seas;
Sweeter than honey of Mellona's bees;
Swifter in flight to you than wingèd fire—
How, then, could language compass such desire?

Song.

WHEN OUR PRINCE CAME HOME.

Broke the gladsome day in glory,
   When our Prince came home;
Broke in flame the headlands hoary,
   When our Prince came home.
On the happy winds our streamers
Swept from towers, ships, and steamers,
And our big guns woke the dreamers,
   When our Prince came home.

Clash'd the bells from every steeple,
   When our Prince came home;
While the cheers of Britain's people,
   When our Prince came home,

Clave the listening air asunder,
Woke the echoes with their thunder,
Woke the whole wide world in wonder,
    When our Prince came home.

'Warm the welcome true and loyal,
    When our Prince came home;
Like himself, free, frank, and royal,
    When our Prince came home.
Dangers dared by land and ocean,
With a patriot's deep devotion,
Woke the breath of our emotion,
    When our Prince came home.

Every hand was raised to greet him,
    When our Prince came home;
All our love went forth to meet him,
    When our Prince came home;
For his noble brave endeavour
East and West to link together
In our hearts sank deep for ever,
    When our Prince came home.

MY LOVE IS A FLOWER.

My Love is a flower
   Amid the leaves sleeping;
I, the air round her bower,
   Guard the sleep of my flower,
   Dry the tears of each hour,
   And the night-dews of weeping.
O my Love is a flower
   Amid the leaves sleeping!

My Love is a linnet
   In golden furze nesting;
I, her mate, every minute
   By the nest of my linnet,
   Sing songs to her in it,
   Sing songs to her, resting.
O my Love is a linnet
   In golden furze nesting!

My Love is a peach
   All the sunbeams are kissing;
I am jealous of each
   For kissing my peach;
   Mine the hand that can reach,
   And she soon will be missing.
O my Love is a peach
   All the sunbeams are kissing!

My Love is a maiden
   With glint-o'-gold tresses;
Just an angel from Aidenn
   Is my faery-sweet maiden;
   I, her lover, am laden
   With a lover's caresses.
O my Love is a maiden
   With glint-o'-gold tresses!

SYMPATHY.

How shall I breathe to thee
　　From my worn heart,
Words of sweet sympathy,
Thoughts that shall solace thee
　　In thy hard part?
How shall I preach to thee
　　The sacred strain;
Tell thee, thy loss is gain;
Tell thee, thy grief is joy;
Tell thee, thou'lt meet thy boy
　　In Heaven again?
This part is not for me,
Mine, silently shall be,
　　To weep with thee.

When slips away
The dreary day
Behind the rounded hills, and solemn night,
Enthroned amid her stars of argent light,
Rules the still world—the mourner's cherish'd hour,
Sacred to grief, and that mysterious power
Which we call memory—
Then, my part shall be
To weep with thee.

When thou, bereft of sleep,
Shalt prayerful vigil keep,
And, peering in the gloom
Of thy encurtain'd room,
Shalt see, in vision-wise, his little cot,
Shalt hear his evening prayer,
And kiss his forehead fair,
Stroke his yellow hair,
Then listen for thy darling's sleeping breath,
Now hush'd in death;
And when Reality, with stony eyes,
Sits on thy couch, and thou dost realise
The dread decree—
" Thou shalt go to him, but he
Shall not, shall not return to thee;"
When the fountains of thy woe
Thine eyelids overflow,

Drenching thy pillow in a bitter sea,
Then will I think of thee,
Then my part shall be
To weep with thee.

Weep, 'twill ease thy pain;
Tears are the kindly rain
By Heaven sent
To moisten our hard hearts beneath its sky,
Lest they should shrink, and shrivel, and be dry;
Lest the white blooms of Charity should die,
Faded and spent.
Oh! there is joy in sadness,
There is bliss in tears—
Amid the summer showers,
The archéd bow appears—
A promise gleaming through the mists of years,
In characters that burn and glow—
Sorrow shall cease—tears shall not always flow.

ENDEAVOUR.

Go forward, strive, and nobly show
　　On the battlefield of life,
That whosoe'er may be the foe
　　Thou'rt equal to the strife.
Thy heart is warm, thy arm is strong,
　　Thou soar'st on eager wings—
Fear not, the harp will give her song,
　　If we rightly touch the strings.

THE LAY OF NOBODY.

In Demogorgon's reign, long years gone by,
  When gods and goddesses dwelt on this earth,
When Cybele's fair mountain pierced the sky,
  So ancient legends say, I had my birth.
It happen'd thus:—An oracle foretold
That if the monarch dug with spade of gold
Beneath a twisted thorn, some centuries old,
        Deep under ground,
        And round and round,
  A wondrous baby would be found.

The mighty monarch bared his kingly arm,
And with the golden spade essay'd the charm;
The stubborn earth gave way to left and right,
Rocks, rent and riven by the monarch's might,

L

Roll'd down the echoing hills, till yawning wide
A chasm open'd in the mountain side;
The old tree groan'd, and moan'd, and creak'd in
    pain,
The wind sobb'd through the boughs, the tender
    rain
Came down in tear-drops; still the glowing King
Delved with a will, and thus did blithely sing—

    " A delver am I—ha, ha!
      In the earth beneath the sun,
   Happy am I, ha, ha!
      For my work is bravely done.
   'Tis good to dig, dig, dig,
      Out of the heat and cold;
And hurrah for the spade that can dig, dig, dig,
    The spade of the yellow gold!"

    " A delver am I—ha, ha!
      Under the pleasant ground,
   Happy am I, ha, ha!
      As I dig round and round.
   Oh fat is the earth to dig, dig, dig,
      In riches to have and hold;
And hurrah for the spade that can dig, dig, dig,
    The spade of the yellow gold!"

The monarch paused, and prest his streaming brow—
" A baby-ruler is the prize—I vow,
   Ye gods! I'll win it!"
    With might and main
    He delved again;
Then listen'd in the cleft to catch some sound.
It came—at last! success his labours crown'd,
    O golden minute!
He search'd his self-wrought cave—and found—
    Nobody in it.

So underneath that gnarled and twisted thorn,
Nobody saw the light, and I was born.

The gods in conclave then, to mark my birth,
    Gave me as dower,
    The wide-wing'd power,
    To rule, and school,
   And sometimes fool the earth;
But, harsh condition, on my shoulders hurl'd
Full half the crimes and blunders of the world.

Supine the monarch lay on throne of state,
Attendant gods around his footstool wait;
From labour resting, calm as night was he,
His vacant eyes, half closed, beholding me.

Then one, with low obeisance, straight began—
"Great Sire of earth—the creature, known as man,
Will chaunt the praises of this quest of thine;
Will grave, in future days, the golden line
In which a world thy attributes may scan.
I draw aside the veil.   Behold the sea!
The seething waters of futurity!
    Across the billowy road I gaze,
A myriad voices thus attune thy praise."

    "O Demogorgon! ruler of the earth!
        Who underground,
        Nobody found,
    And gave Nobody birth,
All hail to thee for thy great quest—
Nobody hast thou loved, Nobody blest,
    Nobody help'd, Nobody raised,
    Nobody cheer'd, Nobody praised;
Through all thy days, Nobody's friend hast stood,
And with thy gold hast done Nobody good."

The monarch smiled his thanks.   The gods dispersed,
In knots and groups my varied points rehearsed.
Said one—"His face is like a sun's—high-brow'd,
What time the sun is hidden by a cloud."
And one—"His voice is sweet as song of bird,
Or laugh of waters by the sleepers heard."

A third—"The spell of form and shape I find
Within the rushing vortex of his mind."
To whom—a youthful god—"This morn I caught
His clear-cut face, in woven mists inwrought
With sudden phantasies of glowing thought,
As one who, looking through the night, sees nought."
Whereat the goddesses upon the air
Flung rhythmic flatteries, and lightly sware,
Compared with them, that Nobody was fair.

Smile, sweet Enchantress! as I wake the string,
Myself the burthen of the song I sing;
The poet's lyre adorn with myrtle sprays,
Beguile my fancy up thy mist-crown'd ways
As, critic-like, I spread the praise.
        Of Nobody.

            Great and strong,
        Mighty powers to me belong
            Over earth and sky,
            And the forces that lie
        In nature and god-like mind.
        Nobody human thought can bind,
            And if it pleasure be,
        Fierce human will, as a lion tamed,
            Can lead in captivity;

Can quench in the hearts of the young and free
 The light of love and of liberty.
The secrets of nature, as time flows on,
  I gather as shells by the sea—
   While the secrets of men,
    Are within my ken,
    Though hidden they be.
I mount and I fly on Fancy's wings,
So list to the melody Nobody sings.

   High, high!
  Nobody can fly
  In the liquid air,
  'Neath the azure sky—
Nobody can sail on the clouds outroll'd
In waves of crimson and burnish'd gold;
The mountains o'ertop where the rivers are born;
Ring the green earth, while the amber morn
Slips through the bars of the star-gemm'd night;
  And shadowless, bright,
Flash through the zones on a shaft of light.

   Fire, fire!
  Nobody can live
  In the furnace fire,
And laugh as the flames mount higher and higher;

Can handle live coals, as a child at play
With the daisies of March or the roses of May—
Can track the red flame to the home of its birth
In the central fires of the globèd earth ;
And 'mid the volcano's fierce sulphurous play,
Can mount on the lava and soar away—
                Away, and away,
Where human foot never hath sullied the clay,
            Where the flowers all day
            With the little winds play,
            And the winds, all the hours,
            Kiss the mouths of the flowers,
        And carry their love-breath away—
                There, flying, I stray,
                Light-hearted and gay,
As an iris-wing'd Psyche of Castalay.

                The sea, the sea !
                The grey-green sea,
        Nobody can live 'neath the rolling sea,
                In the fathomless deeps
                Where the mermaiden sleeps,
                By the rocks brown and bare
                Where she combeth her hair ;
                'Mid the billows' white foam,
                Where she maketh her home,—

And down, down,
Where the seaweed brown
Waves like a wood in the fields of the sea;
In the pink-coral caves,
In the nest of the waves,
There Nobody loves to be.

The Pole, the Pole!
Nobody has found that mystic goal,
Has climb'd its ice-walls stair by stair—
Nor penguin nor seal haunts its desolate shore,
No petrel shrieks in its gelid air—
The albatross will not venture there—
But the wild winds howl, and the tempests pour,
The ice-floes grind, and crash, and roar,
And I and death reign evermore.

Air, water, fire, my will obey,
Their viewless ministrants I lead;
The future, as a scroll, I read,
I make the fleeting present stay.

I track within the vale of time
That future veil'd in mist and rain,
I count its argosies of pain,
And catch the music of its rhyme.

I sail across its sullen seas,
   And dip adown its nether world,
   And know, before my sails are furl'd,
The gulf and all its mysteries.

Nobody sees the nameless graves
   By ocean hid, by forest gloom'd,
   Sees one, in growing snow entomb'd,
Fold unto fold, where winter raves—

His grave who call'd his seamen forth,
   Who pass'd the eternal Arctic gate,
   And on by many a frozen strait,
And bitter winding of the North ;

Who sought to find the farthest shore,
   And found the end of all his days,
   And sleeps within the silent ways,
Where only God had moved before.

    Ah me, Time goes,
     Its dark sea flows ;
   As its waves roll outward
     My knowledge grows.
  Hearken thou, before its close,
  And learn the things Nobody knows.

Nobody knows
When the iron-shod heel of the despot Might
Shall trample no more the form of Right.

Nobody knows
When the sordid souls of the young and old
Shall cease to bow down to the idol Gold;
Deeming not then, what they cannot endure,
As the worst of all crimes, the crime to be poor.

Nobody knows
When Truth, as the lily, shall bloom on high,
When the weeds of the False shall wither and die
Nobody knows.

Nobody knows
When knowledge shall spread like a flood, in its
     might,
Flushing the dark of the world with light,
Turning the many from wrong to the right.

Nobody knows
When pestilence, madness, and famine shall seem
Distorted scenes of a long past dream.

Nobody knows
When the blood-drench'd wars of the world shall
 cease,
And the nations drink health at the waters of
 Peace.

Nobody knows
When drunkenness, poverty, hunger, and crime,
Shall slip from the world, and a glorious time
Shall fall, like a light from a golden clime,
Wrapping the earth in a rest sublime,
  Nobody, Nobody knows!

PRINTED BY BALLANTYNE, HANSON AND CO.
EDINBURGH AND LONDON.

A step—he comes! Alas! 'tis gone—
    It passes by the gate;
Some weary peasant trudging home—
    Lie still, poor heart, and wait!

"How weirdly loom the poplars tall!
    The passion-flowers o'erhead
Are trembling, yet I feel no wind;
    And now a bloom falls dead.
The farthest darkness seems to take
    Strange shapes that cheat the eye;
The very silence throbs with sounds—
    I listen, and they die.
He said, 'I will return ere dark;'
    He told me not to fear.
The dark has come, the stars are out,
    But Albert is not here.

'Why comes he not? I know he seeks
    The Duke, his haughty sire,
Duke Ernest, stern, they say, and proud,
    Of fierce and vengeful ire;
And he will tell of all our love,
    How he woo'd and won his bride,
And I shall ride in cloth-of-gold,
    A lady by his side;

For ere he left he kiss'd me thrice,
    And press'd me to his heart—
' Sweet Agnes, till our days be done
    No power shall make us part ;
And by my knightly faith I swear
    That thou shalt take thy stand
Before the world, my wedded wife,
    The proudest in the land !'
These were his words, his last loved words—
    Why is my heart not light ?
Why sits a fear of coming woe
    Upon my soul to-night?
The air seems stirr'd with viewless wings,
    My senses creep with dread ;
Is it the pulsing of my heart,
    Or did I hear his tread ?
He said ' I will return ere dark ; '
    He told me not to fear :
The dark has come, the moon is up,
    But Albert is not here.

" He comes ! he comes ! my own ! my life !
    Fly, laggard love, be fleet !
But hark ! What means this sound of tongues,
    This noise of many feet ?
Why comes he not alone to-night ? "
    But ere her words had died,

www.ingramcontent.com/pod-product-compliance
Lightning Source LLC
Chambersburg PA
CBHW030558040726
47497CB00008B/2783